J. Nathan

Edited by Stephanie Elliot

Cover Design by Y'all. That Graphic.

Cover Photo by Michelle Lancaster @lanefotograf

Cover Model Dylan Bampton

First Edition June 2024

*For my son. Thank you for adding so much joy,
laughter, and baseball to my life.*

I climbed the stairs to the second floor of our Cape Cod beach house, tugging my suitcase behind me and making quite a racket. It was a wonder no one came out to help me—or greet me for that matter.

The only thing that gave me any comfort returning to this house was sitting on my balcony overlooking the Atlantic Ocean and our own private beach. Since my father was drafted to Boston when I was one, we lived on the Cape from May to August—almost the entire baseball season. And I'd loved it. That is until last summer when I swore never to return.

I stepped inside my room, finding everything the way I'd left it last summer. My white walls were filled with paintings of different ocean views, but the view I loved most was just beyond the French doors. I released my suitcase and moved to the doors, opening them so I could step out onto my balcony and breathe in the ocean air.

I gasped.

A naked girl straddled a naked guy in the Adirondack chair on my balcony.

"What the hell?!" I screeched.

The girl jumped up, grabbing a beach towel and wrapping it around herself. The guy didn't move, staring out at the ocean and not bothering to look to me—or cover up for that matter.

"Get out of my room!" I screamed at both of them.

Her eyes jumped to his. "I thought this was your room?"

"It is," he said.

I pointed my index finger in the direction of my door. "Get out!"

"Your father wouldn't appreciate you talking to me that way," he said, slow and menacing.

"He knows there's a strange guy in *my* room?" I asked dubiously.

"Been here for almost a month." He finally stood. He was nearly a foot taller than me, and I did what I could to meet his blue gaze under a ruffled head of dirty blond hair. "Get used to it. I'm here all summer."

I kept my eyes focused on his since he was still naked, and there was no way I'd give him the satisfaction of looking down. "This is *my* room."

"Gonna have to talk to Daddy then because he said it was mine."

"Over my dead body," I growled.

His eyes moved down my body in a slow appraisal. "Won't be a loss." He stepped around me and finally grabbed a towel. He wrapped it around his hips then grabbed a ball cap and lowered it over his messy hair, walking out of my room with the girl and slamming the door behind them.

Dammit!

I should've known my father, a retired professional baseball player, would've taken in a college baseball player.

Especially, since I was supposed to be backpacking around Europe all summer. I guess no one thought my trip would be cut short since I'd been saving up to go all year—working my ass off at the school bookstore so I wouldn't have to ask my parents for a penny.

Seething, I stepped out onto my balcony. I couldn't help looking to the chair. Anger gnawed at my insides. I bent down and grasped the chair with both hands, somehow lifting the heavy thing and launching it over the deck railing. The wood planks splintered and shattered all over the patio below.

"You better replace my chair," the guy called as he and the girl stepped around the mess and walked by the pool, past the pool house, and through the path to *my* beach.

"Wouldn't sit in that trash if you paid me!" I yelled before spinning around and slamming my French doors shut.

For the first time in my life, I closed the white curtains to keep out the normally breathtaking view. He could have the beach for now. But he couldn't have my room.

I stormed into the kitchen and found my father seated at a stool at the center island. "Who is he?"

"Peyton!" My father jumped up and hugged me. "You're home?"

"Clearly," I said not bothering to return his hug. "Where's Mom?"

A strange look flittered across his face.

"I said, 'Where's Mom?'"

"She decided to spend some time with Grandma."

"How long has she been gone?" I asked since she hadn't mentioned it in any of her check-in texts while I was away.

He shrugged.

"Well, when will she be back?" I pressed, not wanting

to be alone with him for the remainder of the summer.

"You'll have to ask her," he said offhandedly, but I could tell he had no idea and it probably drove him nuts.

"I take it she didn't want to come back here either," I said.

"You seem a little jet lagged," he said.

"I'm not jet lagged," I snapped. "I'm pissed that you gave my room away."

"I didn't give your room away," he explained. "The bathroom in the guest room was being remodeled. I told him to take your room since you were supposed to be gone all summer. Why *are* you home early?"

"I needed the beach," I clipped, not bothering to mention Mel meeting a guy and abandoning me in Amsterdam. "Just so you know, your baseball player's a pig. Did you know he had a girl in my room with him?"

"Crew's twenty-one," my father said, as if that was explanation enough.

"Crew?" I scoffed. "What kind of name is that?"

"He's the star on the Sharks. We're his host family. If that's what he wants to do on his day off, that's not for us to say."

"You'd know."

He ignored my comment and moved to the refrigerator, grabbing a beer.

"Well, you need to tell him he can't stay in my room."

"No can do," he said before taking a long pull of his beer. "You're the one who showed up here unannounced. Your paths were never meant to cross."

"Well, now they have."

"Listen, I'm doing sports analysis for the Sox," he explained. "I'm gone for days at a time. I need to know you're not gonna cause a problem."

"*You* caused the problem."

"Hey, Mr. Richmond," a deep voice said.

I spun around. Crew entered alone in a bathing suit and sleeveless shirt.

"How many times do I have to tell you to call me Marty," my father said to him.

I rolled my eyes.

"This must be your daughter," Crew said.

"This is Peyton," my father explained. "She surprised us by coming back early from Europe."

Crew smirked. "Nice to meet you, Peyton."

"You can drop the act. He's well aware that we've already met," I said. "Did you contaminate my beach too?"

Crew choked, surprised by my candor, but he recovered like players always did. "Kept it to a minimum."

"I need you to get your stuff out of my room," I said.

"Now wait a minute, Peyton," my father said. "I never said I was relocating Crew. He's our guest."

Crew crossed his arms, his smug eyes narrowing on mine.

"Why don't you take the guest room," my father said, pulling my attention to him. "The bathroom's finished now."

"The guest room doesn't have an ocean view," I countered.

"Crew's a guest," my father said, pegging me with his eyes. "We always treat our guests with hospitality."

Feeling my anger growing, I spun away from them. "Screw this." I stormed out of the house, making my way around the pool, past the pool house, and to the sandy path. I needed my beach. I needed to be away from a man who I despised and a guy who I'd likely punch in the face if he didn't erase that smug look from it.

CHAPTER TWO

I trudged through the sand in my sneakers, finding a spot on the beach just out of reach from the waves to sit. I slipped my phone from my pocket and called my mom.

She picked up on the first ring. "Peyton?"

"Mom?"

"Are you okay?" she asked.

"Are *you*?"

She was slow to respond. "I'm getting there."

"I wish I'd known you weren't here..."

"I'm sorry for that," she said.

"I would've flown to Alabama," I explained. "I still can."

"I know. But...I think you and your father have some unresolved issues that you need to work out."

"You set me up?" I asked, unable to believe she'd do something like that to me. I was just as hurt as she was.

"I couldn't bring myself to go back there," she admitted. "I need time."

I closed my eyes. The pain in her voice broke my heart. "I understand."

"I love you, Honey," my mom said.

"I love you, too," I said before switching off my phone.

I lay back on the sand unsure how to feel about what she'd said. I knew my father and I had unresolved issues. But if I wanted to resolve them, I would have shown up for Thanksgiving or come home for Christmas break or arrived in May when my junior year ended instead of going overseas.

But I hadn't.

Because I didn't want to resolve the issues.

"Peyton?"

I sat up as my next-door neighbor Gina hurried out from her path. We'd grown up together at the beach. She'd been my partner in crime over the years. And though we clicked over our love for the beach, we were as opposite as they came. I was Chucks and band T-shirts, and she was wedges and sundresses.

"What are you doing here?" she asked, sitting down beside me and tucking her sundress under her as she did. She'd cut her long dark hair to her shoulders and it looked curlier than it had over the years. "I thought you were going to be gone all summer?"

"Long story."

"Is everything okay? Are *you* okay?" she asked, always concerned about me.

"Aside from finding out my mom's in Alabama and my room's been given away, I've never been better," I lied.

She winced. "If it's any consolation, *I'm* happy you're here."

"That bad without me?" I asked.

"You have no idea," she said.

I stared out at the waves, realizing how much I missed the ocean while I was overseas.

"So, tell me why you're back," Gina pressed.

I sifted sand through my fingers. "Well, I expected gorgeous scenery, amazing food, and an epic love story sweeping countries."

"*And?*" she prompted.

"And, what I got was dirty hostels, too much food, and no love story."

"That sucks."

"Not for Mel. She met an Italian guy and took off with him once we reached Amsterdam."

Her eyes widened. "Seriously?"

I nodded.

"I'm sorry. I know you never wanted to be back under the same roof as—"

"Had I known my mother was with my grandmother, I would've flown to Alabama instead. I still might."

"But I just got you back," Gina argued.

"I know, it's just..."

"I understand," Gina said, knowing what I'd been through last summer and why I wouldn't want to return— especially without my mother here. "So, you've met Crew?"

My eyes skipped to hers. "Have you?"

"Just in passing. But I can't say I wouldn't like to get to know him better," she laughed.

"He's a pig," I snapped.

"How do you know?" she asked.

"I walked in on him and some girl."

She wrinkled her nose. "No way."

"It was not the welcome home I expected."

"Are you really gonna leave?" she asked.

I shrugged. "I can't coexist with him."

She didn't ask which one. I guess it was clear I meant

both of them. "I'm sorry," she said, and I couldn't miss the sadness in her tone.

I knew Gina relied on me for her fun over the summer, and up until now, I'd abandoned her. I guess I was no better than Mel. I watched the waves crashing in front of us for a long time. Could I stay for the rest of the summer? Could I avoid my father and Crew? Could I allow myself to be happy in a house that brought back bad memories—at least since last summer? "Let's go out."

Gina's eyes lit up. "What?"

"We'll hit the bars. We deserve a night out."

She smiled, and I could see how grateful she was for the offer.

Even though every part of my body wanted to curl up in bed because I was exhausted, jetlagged, and pissed I was there and my mom wasn't, I'd do it for Gina.

"Let's meet out front at nine," she said, pushing herself to her feet.

"Okay," I said, standing up beside her.

We parted ways by the path. I headed to my back patio, stopping where the broken chair should've been. I twisted around, seeking any of its remnants, but someone had cleaned it up.

I could see my father through the kitchen windows. In no mood for another run-in, I circled the house to the front door, climbed the stairs to the second floor, and headed to get my suitcase from *my* room.

"You people don't knock in this house?"

I stopped short a few feet into my room. Crew lay on my bed staring at the phone in his hand. I huffed my frustration. "Let's get something straight. This is *my* room. And I'm only gonna play nice because...well because I don't need any more aggravation here." I snatched up the handle of my suitcase and rolled it into *my* bathroom. If he thought I'd be giving up that easily, he was sorely mistaken. I slammed the bathroom door shut for the whole house to hear and locked it behind me.

I rummaged through my suitcase for a clean shirt and cutoffs. There wasn't a chance in hell I was leaving this bathroom until I was clean and dressed for a night out. If he needed it, *he* could use the guest bathroom.

In the shower, I let the water rain over me for a long time. The water pressure overseas was lacking the power I needed. I lifted Crew's bottle of shampoo to my nose. Sandalwood. Figures. I placed it back down and used my own products on my hair and body, then grabbed a towel from the white linen chest.

After I dried off, I shimmied into my shirt and cutoffs. As my hair dried, I could see the beachy waves return. I'd been accustomed to just pulling it up in a ponytail when I was in Europe, so I'd forgotten how nice it felt to wear it down. I brushed on minimal makeup and slipped on my flip-flops. It was eight-thirty, so I closed my suitcase and opened the door. Crew wasn't in my room when I stepped out.

Smart move on his part.

CHAPTER THREE

"You clean up well," Gina teased as I met her at the end of my gravel driveway.

My eyes drifted over her sundress and wedges. "One of us has to look presentable."

She laughed as our Uber pulled up, and we slipped into the backseat.

"Monty's, right?" I asked her.

"Of course," she said with a grin.

We'd been getting into Monty's with fake IDs since we were seventeen. Now, we were legit twenty-one-year-olds. After a short drive along the coast, our driver dropped us in front of the beachside bar. We showed the bouncer our IDs and slipped inside to grab a drink. The place was pretty busy for a Wednesday night. But, then again, most people were vacationing, so the days of the week on the Cape were irrelevant. We wove our way through the tables until we reached the bar. The bartender lifted her chin in my direction.

"Two Coronas," I called before scanning the bar for familiar faces. Most looked like tourists. A group of guys near the pool table caught my attention. They were around our age but didn't pay us the least bit of attention.

The bartender returned with the beers, and I paid before we walked out to the back deck. Tiki torches surrounded the deck, and big bulb lights were strung every which way above our heads. I leaned against the railing and gazed out at the ocean. The roar of the waves was more prominent in the darkness. "It's so beautiful at night," I mused. "I really missed this."

"You sure you want to leave?" she asked.

"I don't want to leave. I think I need to leave."

An older guy wearing a straw hat stepped up, leaning against the railing beside us. "Hey, ladies. You come here often?"

I looked to Gina. "Is he serious?"

She stifled a grin.

"Of course I'm serious," he said, a slight slur to his words.

"Sorry to break it to you," I said. "But that pick-up line went out with the denim shorts you're wearing."

He glanced down at his shorts. "The guy at the store said they were vintage."

I winced. "He played you, dude."

He shook his head and walked away.

"Not everyone can afford to pull off the ridiculously-expensive-but-trying-to-look-like-a-beach-bum-look   you're sporting," a voice nearby said.

I spun around. Crew stood behind me sipping a beer. His eyes were nearly concealed by the Sharks ball cap he wore low on his head, his messy hair peeking out all around it. My teeth clenched. "Oh, I'm sorry. I didn't realize we were pointing out other people's indiscretions. Have we hit that point in our relationship already?"

"You don't need to be such a bitch. The guy clearly thought you were cute and wanted to talk to you."

"Just because someone wants to talk to me doesn't mean I wanna talk to them," I challenged. "Case in point."

Crew's jaw ticked as if dealing with me was so difficult. "You're no better than him. You're no better than anyone."

"Excuse me?" I said.

"Nope. Excuse me." He turned away from us and headed inside the bar.

"Holy shit," Gina said.

My eyes jumped to hers. "What?"

"He's even better looking up close."

I hitched my thumb over my shoulder. "That's what you took away from that?"

She shrugged guiltily. "I didn't hear much. I was staring at his blue eyes and chiseled jaw line."

I rolled my eyes. Good looks meant nothing. All they did was conceal lies and mask deceit.

Gina and I spent most of the night on the patio, avoiding straw hat guy and asshole ball players. I filled Gina in on all the places I'd traveled while abroad, my phone call with my mom, *and* my current room situation.

"Sounds like *both* of your parents made decisions for you," she said.

"I'm an adult. They can't tell me what to do."

Gina stifled a smile.

"What?"

"Ironically, you sound very much like a little kid right now."

I tilted my head to the side. "You know you're one of the only people on this planet I'd let speak to me that way, right?"

She pressed her hand to her heart. "Honored."

I took a swig of my beer to conceal my grin.

"Seriously, though, I think you and Crew need to get whatever's going on figured out before it gets worse," she offered.

"You know what? That's a great idea." I moved to the deck bar and ordered a couple tequila shots. I handed Gina one and lifted mine into the air. "To another amazing summer."

"To another amazing summer," she repeated before we downed our shots, the straight alcohol burning a path down my throat.

"Now, let's go inside," I said, starting to feel the effects of all the alcohol I'd drank.

"Oh," Gina said, finally catching on to my true intent. "That's probably not the best idea," she called, following after me.

"It was *your* idea," I reminded her.

"But I didn't mean right now."

We pushed our way through the people congregating inside as I searched for Crew. I could see the group of guys still playing pool in the corner of the room, and I wondered if I'd missed him when we first arrived.

As we neared the group, I realized they all wore Sharks ball caps and were all six feet or taller. All built. All pretty damn good looking. I made my way over to the pool table, eyeing the girls hanging around them. *Damn groupies.* The Cape League was an invite only baseball league made up of college players who had a shot at making it to the major leagues. Not all of them would get drafted, but some definitely would. That meant they needed to beware of groupies looking to latch on to them for what they could become—and possess. And, these girls would go to great lengths to get them.

"Hey beautiful," one of the guys said.

I rolled my eyes, in no mood for more lame pick-up lines.

"Hi," Gina said, eating up the lines.

She was allowed to fall for them. I just wouldn't be susceptible to ball players' shady ways.

"Haven't seen you two around here before," the guy said. "You tourists?"

"Nope. We're locals," Gina explained. "Peyton just returned from backpacking around Europe. We needed a night out to celebrate."

"Europe, huh?" he asked me. "How was that?"

"Well, there were no baseball players around, so there was that."

"*Peyton*," Gina chided under her breath.

"What?" I asked innocently. "Just making an observation."

"You guys play for the Sharks?" she asked him, even though his hat answered her question.

"Yup," he said with a grin displaying two front teeth slightly bigger than the rest. "We're undefeated."

I scoffed.

"Don't you like baseball?" he asked me.

"I love baseball. Just not the players," I said.

"Noted." His eyes shifted back to Gina. "Can I get you a drink?"

She nodded, seemingly just as put off by my bad attitude as he was. She followed him to the bar, and I was left to stand awkwardly alone.

"If you were going for the everyone-stay-the-hell-away-from-me-because-I'm-a-bitch routine, you nailed it," Crew said, materializing beside me.

"Good. Wouldn't want to catch anything from any of you," I said.

"Oh, rest assured. None of us would touch you."

"Perfect."

He looked at me with disdain. "Why don't you head home. Wouldn't want you bringing your negativity near my teammates."

"I'll go home when I want to go home," I said. "And I'm not the one with a curfew."

"Yeah, but you're the one who acts like they need one." He turned away from me and walked over to an empty chair near the pool table. As soon as he sat, a girl found her way onto his lap. And she wasn't the girl from earlier. *Pig.*

She smirked my way, telling me she thought getting his attention would piss me off.

Nope. You can have him. Just not in my room.

I turned away from them and found Gina and the ball player at the bar.

"You want a drink?" he offered, though I sensed he only did it to gain brownie points with Gina.

"No. I'm fine," I said.

"You know Crew?" he asked, clearly having seen us talking.

"My family's hosting him," I explained.

"Your dad's Marty Richmond?" Excitement radiated off him like all of my father's fans.

"The one and only," I said, less than pleased to have to admit it.

"Dude's a legend," he said. "I cried when he retired."

I didn't respond.

"I asked Crew to get me an autograph," he continued, "but he hasn't yet."

"Maybe Gina can bring you over to the house," I offered.

Gina's eyes got all big, knowing I was a true wingman—when I wasn't being such a bitch. "Sure," she said.

He smiled, and I knew I just assured Gina that she'd be seeing Mr. Ball Player again.

"I'm gonna head out," I told her.

Her face dropped as if it was the last thing she wanted to do.

"You stay," I assured her. "I need to walk."

"You sure?" she asked, though I knew she didn't want to leave with me.

"Have fun. I'll talk to you tomorrow."

CHAPTER FOUR

I left Gina and the ball player at the bar and made my way out front. It was a gorgeous night, and I hadn't been lying when I said I needed to walk. I hadn't realized how much anger I'd been harnessing since arriving to the Cape. I began the trek down the deserted coastal road—probably not my best decision. But then again, coming to the beach, after I'd sworn never to step foot back in the house again, had been even worse.

My mind traveled back to last summer. To the knock on the door. To the twenty-something woman standing there with a five-year-old little girl holding her hand. To the screams of my mother. To the apologies of my father. To the disgust in my mother's eyes. To the slamming of doors. To the tears shed. To the silence in the house for the last month of summer. To the hatred I felt toward my father—the man who single-handedly destroyed our family. To the disappointment I felt toward my mother because she stayed with him.

I wondered all year how many other women he'd been with. How many other children existed because my father had cheated on my mother. I knew I'd never be able to look him in the eyes again and see the man I idolized. I knew I'd never be able to forgive him for the weak man he truly was.

When I left last August, I didn't bother saying goodbye, but it *had been* goodbye. At least, I thought it had been. I never planned to be under the same roof as my father again. And, while it might've been unfair, I viewed my mother differently too. How could she ever forgive him? Trust him? Love him?

He'd betrayed her.

He'd betrayed *us*.

If it were me, I would've left his ass and taken all of his money.

But my mother wasn't me.

Though, her distancing herself from him this summer told me something was going on with her. I hoped she knew that trying to force me to forgive him wouldn't make it better. It wouldn't make all the pain go away. Because, truth be told, I had no desire to forgive him. I hoped she divorced him. It was for the best.

When I reached the house, it was shrouded in darkness. I walked around to the back patio door. I slipped inside and crept upstairs, not wanting to run into my father. I twisted the knob on my door and slipped inside my room, closing the door behind me. Shit! I wasn't staying in my room. I began to twist the doorknob to leave but stopped.

Crew wasn't back yet.

And, this *was* my room.

I stripped out of my shorts, staying in my T-shirt and panties. I peeled back the comforter on my bed and slipped under the sheets. I fluffed the pillow under my head and turned onto my side toward the French doors. With the curtains open, I could see the stars filling the night sky. My heavy lids told me the stars would be the last thing I saw before exhaustion mixed with the liquor I'd consumed pulled me under.

————

In my dream, I was a little girl again. Splashing water as I ran, trying to avoid the waves. Laughing uncontrollably. Thrust into the air in my father's arms. The sunlight shined on my sun-kissed cheeks. Seagulls squawked, soaring over-head. Life couldn't get any sweeter. I loved when he had a day off from baseball because he could stay with us all day and night. He spun me around, and I spread my arms, flying like one of the seagulls.

Footsteps in the hallway pulled me from my dream.

Though I didn't face the door, I heard the knob rattle and the door open. I lay still, waiting for Crew to notice me there. He'd be pissed, but he'd turn around and head to the guest room where he belonged.

I waited.

His feet shuffled then the door closed.

I stifled a smile. I'd won.

"So that we're clear," he said, his deep voice startling me still. "I'm not leaving."

I didn't say anything, but I could hear him shucking off his shoes and shedding his clothes. He walked toward the bed and then pulled back the comforter and sheet.

Shit.

Was he looking at me? My panties left little to the imag-ination.

He slipped underneath the sheets, and with both of us in the bed there was little room to move. He turned onto his side, but I wasn't sure which way he turned until he spoke and it wasn't directly in my ear. "I know you're awake."

I didn't respond.

"This is the room I was given, and it's the room I'm staying in. So, we can keep on playing this little who-gets-to-the-room-first game, but I'm not going anywhere."

"I could lock the door," I finally said.

"Are you five?" he countered.

Asshole.

"If your father finds you in here, I'm telling him you snuck in and tried to sleep with me."

"Or, I could tell him you gave up the room only to slip in during the middle of the night to sleep with *me*."

"Like that would ever happen."

I resisted the urge to use my nails. "Yeah, I'm definitely not the slutty type you're into."

He scoffed.

"And consider yourself warned. If your hand crosses the middle of the bed, I will use my knee where it'll hurt." He didn't bother responding, and I didn't give him the satisfaction of another word. I was holding my own and not budging. I wondered how long I could go without moving. Could I lay this still all night? Could he? That was the last thought that crossed my mind before sleep pulled me back under.

CHAPTER FIVE

I rolled over and flopped right onto my stomach. I cracked my eyes to discover sunlight filling my room and Crew not in the bed. I lifted my head, but he wasn't in the room or the bathroom. Had he gone to the guest room after I fell asleep? Had he woken before me and slipped out?

I climbed out from under the sheets and sat on the edge of the bed. The amount of alcohol I consumed left a dull ache in my temples and fuzziness in my brain. I pushed myself to my feet and padded my way over to the bathroom. I flinched when I caught sight of myself in the mirror. My mascara had smudged around my eyes, and my hair was matted to one side of my head. Nice.

From the sink vanity, I grabbed his tube of toothpaste, squirted some on my finger, and swished it around in my mouth with some sink water. As I spit it out, I noticed a pair of tweezers. Of course, Crew was the type of guy to manscape.

I shed my clothes and stepped into my shower. The spray of water and steam worked wonders to relieve my headache. And, after a nice long shower, I stepped out, wrapped a towel around me, and grabbed my dirty clothes as I made my way into the hallway.

"Peyton?"

I spun around to find my father standing there.

"What are you doing in there?" he asked.

"Crew wasn't here so I figured I'd use my shower." It wasn't all a lie.

"He's out for a run, but I told you the guest bathroom is finished," he said.

I shrugged. "I chose not to listen. Are you gonna punish me?"

He huffed his frustration. "Is that what you want?"

"I don't want anything from you. I just need a place to stay until school starts."

"Oh, you mean the school your mother and I pay for?" He scoffed as if his intent wasn't clear enough.

"Are we done here?"

He stepped to the side of the hall so I could pass by.

I walked around him, careful not to touch any part of him.

"I'm not the enemy," he mumbled once I was past him.

"Yes, you are," I said as I slipped into the guest room and flopped down onto the bed. The pit in my stomach grew every time we spoke. Every time I remembered the type of man he really was.

My phone buzzed and a text appeared on my screen.

Gina: Bonfire tonight after the game. You in?

Me: I take it things went well with you and the ball player?

She sent a heart emoji back.

I laughed to myself. She'd always been corny. It was one of the things I adored about her.

Me: You know I hate baseball players.

Gina: Pleeeeeeaase.

If I said no, I'd be hurting Gina. If I said yes, the night was gonna suck. I sighed.

Me: Fine.

She sent back a kissy face emoji.

I tossed my phone down and climbed under the sheets. I'd avoid the world until I needed to leave for the stupid bonfire.

———

"Peyton!" Gina called.

I twisted from my spot on the sand to see her approaching from the path down to the beach. I'd spent the last hour watching the waves under the light of the full moon. I'd only left my room after I heard my father leaving for the game.

"Have you been out here long?" she asked, tucking her sundress under her before sitting beside me.

I shrugged. "Time stands still out here."

She smiled in agreement.

"I'm surprised you didn't go to the game," I said.

"I thought it might seem too desperate," she admitted.

"He seemed into you," I said, letting my hand drift over the cool grains of sand.

"We've been texting all day," she admitted.

"He obviously realizes you're gorgeous, sweet, funny, and you know baseball. You're the total package."

She glanced up. "You are too."

I shrugged. "Not looking for a prince to sweep me away. Especially a ball player."

She frowned.

I knew they weren't all untrustworthy. But since the man I was supposed to trust implicitly proved to be a deceitful cheater, how would I ever trust some random guy who could crush me without another thought. Especially, when they were only passing through town for a few months. "I'll make you a deal. I'll go to the game tomorrow night, if I can leave the bonfire once the two of you take off to be alone."

She stifled a smile. "Who said we'd take off to be alone?"

I cocked my head.

She smiled. "Deal."

Gina got word that the game ended, so we knew the guys would be arriving to the bonfire site at the other end of the beach within the hour. We stayed where we were for a while then headed down the beach. I slipped off my flip-flops and walked along the surf while Gina walked barefoot, keeping her feet dry.

The bonfire was ablaze when we reached the far side of the beach. Ball players walked around with red cups and girls sat on blankets. I knew the fire would be short-lived. The Cape League instilled a midnight curfew for all play-ers. They played almost every night, so it helped ensure that they didn't go wild while they were here for the summer. That wasn't only out of respect for their host families, but it ensured they wouldn't hurt their performance on the field or their chance of being drafted into the big leagues—if that was in the cards for them.

"Hey!" Gina's baseball player called as he approached

us. His smile faded slightly when he noticed me with her. "Glad you came," he said to Gina.

"I hope you don't mind I brought Peyton," Gina said, likely noticing his displeasure with seeing me there.

"Not at all," he lied.

"I didn't catch your name at the bar," I said, not wanting it to look like Gina had been talking about him.

"Cody," he said. "Can I get you guys a drink?"

Gina nodded. "Sure."

He looked to me.

"Sure."

He ticked his head. "Come on over while I get the drinks."

We followed him to the coolers. I did a quick sweep of the other people there while he poured beer into red cups for us. I recognized some of the guys and girls from the bar. My nemesis was there in a beach chair with a girl on his lap. Because of the smoky haze of the fire, I couldn't tell if she was the one from the bar or the one from my balcony.

"Here you go," Cody said.

"Thanks," I said, taking the red cup from him and staring into the foam of the beer.

"Don't worry. I didn't slip anything into it," he said.

I lifted my eyes to his. "Oh, I didn't think you did."

He smiled. "Totally kidding."

I forced a smile.

He slipped his hand into Gina's. "Come on. I wanna show you something."

She glanced to me guiltily.

"Go," I assured her. "I'm fine."

She smiled her appreciation then let him tug her down to the water.

I stood awkwardly alone, sipping my beer as I watched a couple of guys throw a football while others mingled with local girls I'd recognized from my time there each summer. If they recognized me, they didn't let on—or even look my way. I spotted Crew kissing the girl in his lap. I wondered if she knew he slept in my bed last night. Ugh. I hated that the thought even crossed my mind. It wasn't like either one of us liked it. We both were stubbornly doing what stubborn people did. Push buttons. Stand their ground. Remain unfazed.

"Hey, aren't you Marty Richmond's daughter?" A guy stepped up beside me. He stood at about six four, so I raised my gaze to meet his.

"Uh-huh."

"You don't sound impressed," he said.

"What's your dad's name?" I asked him.

"What?"

"What's your dad's name?" I repeated.

"Buck."

"I hear you're Buck's son," I said.

His eyes narrowed.

"My name's Peyton, and I am far more interesting than who my father is. Just like you are far more interesting than being just Buck's son."

"Touché."

I shrugged. "Just gets old."

"Sorry to bring it up, *Peyton*," he said, stressing my name.

"What's your name, Buck's son?"

He chuckled. "Sam."

"Nice to meet you, *Sam*. You play for the Sharks?"

He glanced down at himself. "Did my athletic physique give me away?"

"Totally," I said, playing along since I could sense he wasn't a total douche. "What position do you play?"

"Is this a test?"

My brows lifted. "A test?"

"Yeah. Like if I'm the right-fielder, are you gonna walk away?"

"Well, *are* you the right-fielder?" I asked.

"Yes."

I sipped my beer as he awaited my response. "You passed. I can talk to you."

He laughed. "What position do you have something against?"

"Pitchers and shortstops."

He threw back his head and laughed. "What's wrong with them?"

"We both know what's wrong with them," I said.

"They're more arrogant than the rest of us?" he asked.

"Your words, not mine."

He sipped his drink. "I like you."

"Well, that's unfortunate because I hate baseball players."

"Doesn't seem like you hate me," Sam said.

"I don't hate you *right now*," I said. "But, when you get rich and famous, I will."

"You think I'm good enough to be rich and famous?"

I lifted a shoulder. "Haven't seen you play."

His eyes narrowed. "Wait. You haven't been to any of our games?"

I shook my head. "I just got back from Europe."

"Oh, I think I heard that," he said.

"From who?" I asked.

"Guys gossip more than girls. And, I hear you've got an attitude."

"Then why in the world did you come over here and talk to me?"

"Because I am not opposed to girls with attitudes."

For the first time since arriving in town, laughter rushed out of me. "Oh, so you're that guy?"

"I am definitely that guy," he assured me.

"And not even the shortstop," I mused.

"Not even the shortstop," he agreed.

A comfortable silence passed between us. My eyes shifted down to the water where Cody and Gina stood in the moonlight. Gina was laughing as Cody spoke, and I wondered what he said to make her so happy. "So, what's up with Cody," I asked Sam. "Is he a good guy?"

"Yeah. He's got sisters. Guys with sisters tend to be better guys."

"Do *you* have a sister?"

"Nope."

We both laughed.

He glanced to my cup. "Need another drink?"

I tipped my cup upside down and nothing came out. "Sure."

He hitched his head toward the coolers. I followed him, passing by Crew and a girl I didn't recognize on his lap. I'd like to say I didn't initiate...but I couldn't help myself.

"Just curious," I said, slowing to look the girl in the eyes. "Can you still smell my perfume?"

"What?" she asked, looking me up and down.

I looked to Crew. I expected rage but instead found amusement.

I shrugged. "The guy gets around. And snores." I looked to Sam standing confused beside me. "I'll have that drink now."

"You're not hooking up with Burke, are you?" Sam asked.

"*God*, no. I just like pissing him off."

We grabbed another beer and spent the rest of the night hanging with Gina and Cody away from the others.

Cody checked his phone and panicked. "Shit!"

I looked at my phone and saw it was nearing midnight. "Looks like Cinderella needs to get home." As soon as the words left my lips, my eyes shot to where Crew *had* been sitting. *Dammit.*

I jumped to my feet. "I gotta go, too."

"Cody's gonna bring me home," Gina explained.

"I can drive you," Sam offered.

"Would you mind?" I asked, knowing he'd get me home faster than if I walked.

"Not at all."

"I'll see you tomorrow," I said to Gina before rushing toward the parking lot.

Sam opened the passenger door of an expensive sports car. "Is this yours?" I asked as I slipped into the front seat.

"Nah. My host family's loaded, and they let me use their car," he explained as he shut my door. "Where to?" he asked once he settled into the driver's seat.

"I'm just on the other end of the beach."

He pulled out of the parking lot and we were on our way. "It's beautiful here."

"This is your first time on the Cape League?"

His eyes moved between me and the road. "Yeah. I sucked last year and didn't get invited."

"Ah, so you admit you're not always awesome."

He chuckled. "When are we hanging out again?"

My head swiveled to meet his gaze. "Did I say we were hanging out again?"

"No. But I know we will."

"You know?"

He nodded. "You hate baseball players and I'm not looking for anything with anyone. We're the perfect bromance."

"I'm not a bro."

He laughed. "You know what I mean."

I pointed to my road on the right. "It's that one. But it's a dead end, so don't bother turning. I can hop out here."

"You sure?" he asked as he pulled to a stop.

"Yeah. Thanks for an unexpectedly fun night."

He smirked. "I knew you liked me."

I pushed open the door and stepped out. I leaned back in. "See ya around, Sam."

"We've got another home game tomorrow night. I'll look for you."

I laughed as I shut the door and hurried down my road. I glanced up at my dark house and slipped inside the front door. I tiptoed up the stairs and saw that my door was closed. I held my breath and turned the knob, hoping Crew hadn't beaten me home. Inside, Crew lay in bed, and he appeared to be asleep.

I contemplated my next move. I didn't need to keep up this ridiculous game, but he'd left early to no doubt get home before me. He wanted to know what I'd do. Would I back down now that I had to make the decision? Or, would I rise to the challenge?

No-brainer.

I shed my shoes and shorts so I was in my panties and T-shirt. I padded to the side of the bed that had the most room and placed my phone on the nightstand. I lifted the sheet and climbed underneath carefully, rolling onto my side away from him and tucking my hands beneath my pillow.

I'd give Crew one thing. His annoying presence was keeping my mind off my father.

I thought back to the bonfire. It hadn't been as bad as I thought it would be. I had fun hanging with Sam, Gina, and Cody. And, I got to know Cody more and could see what Gina saw in him. He was a country boy who loved his mama and sisters. He had us laughing all night with stories about mishaps on their farm. Sam too seemed to be a good guy. He was in tears when Cody told his goat story, and it just made me like him more. Maybe I *would* go check out one of their games.

"You sounded jealous," Crew murmured beside me.

I stilled.

"Were you trying to scare other girls away from me?"

"Just thought she should know who she's getting involved with," I replied.

"And who's that?" he challenged.

"A guy who moves from girl to girl," I said.

"Then why imply you were one of those girls?"

"I implied nothing. You sleep in my room that inevitably smells like me. It's not my fault if that's not how she took it."

A long stretch of silence passed.

The crashing of the ocean waves beyond my French doors brought me such comfort. It was my own personal lullaby. And nothing—not my father or jerky baseball players—could ruin that for me.

"Who hurt you?" Crew asked, breaking the quiet in the room.

"What?"

"Your walls are so damn tall and thick. Someone had to have hurt you," he said.

"Why don't you worry about you, and I'll worry about me," I snapped.

He shifted, and though I couldn't see him, I could tell he turned onto his side to face me. "I'm not the asshole you think I am."

"Watch yourself. If any part of your body touches mine—"

"What's wrong? Scared you'll like it?"

I didn't give him the satisfaction of a response.

"We don't have to be enemies."

I let his words hang in the night. Of course we had to be enemies. It was the only way to leave this summer less unscathed than when I arrived.

Not surprising, I woke up alone in my bed. I reached for my phone on the nightstand and found a text from Gina. **Did you hook up with Sam?**

I laughed to myself as I texted my response. **And ruin our newfound bromance? No.**

Gina: LOL. Wanna go to the game with me tonight?

Me: Yes, but only bc I told Sam I might.

Gina: I'll drive. Meet me out front at 5.

Me: K

I finally climbed out of bed around noon and got into the shower. Since my shampoo was in the guest room, I used Crew's, knowing I'd end up smelling like him for the rest of the day. When I stepped out, I grabbed a towel and used it to ring the water from my hair before wrapping it around myself.

I opened the door and froze. Crew lay on my bed with an open book in his hand.

"Fierce, frightening, fabulous...the ocean is," he read.

The blood drained from my face.

"Special, symphonic, solitary...the beach is," he continued.

"Give me that." I moved toward him with my hand out. "It's not yours."

"Enormous, extraordinary, elaborate...the universe is," he read.

I grabbed it out of his hand.

"I didn't know you wrote poetry," he said.

I held the book against my chest. "It's rude to read other people's thoughts without their permission."

"I didn't realize it was private," he said.

"It was buried in the bottom of my closet," I argued.

"Well, maybe it shouldn't be."

I rolled my eyes and walked out.

———

I'd thrown on some jeans, a plain white T-shirt, and a blue camo baseball cap. I met Gina at five and slipped into her car.

"You look ready for a ball game," she said.

"Ready as I'll ever be."

We took the short drive through town until we reached the parking lot for the ball park. For a week night, it was pretty full.

"I brought us chairs," she said, knowing there was a designated area on a grassy hill on the first base line where all the host families sat.

Her family hosted baseball players until Gina turned fifteen. After that, having good-looking college baseball players under the same roof became problematic for her parents. They knew baseball players could turn even the most innocent girl bad.

We unpacked the chairs from her trunk then walked the short distance to the entry. Most people who didn't know the area probably wouldn't have even known the field was behind a set of buildings on the main road. There was no big sign, and certainly no grandstand—just a few bleachers on both sides and lots of grassy areas to sit. Even though some of the guys would be going pro, they weren't there yet, which made the draw for games rather lackluster—but free. They'd get their day, my dad always said. He'd know. He played for almost eighteen years in the big leagues after starting right here in the Cape League where he'd met my mom—a local girl—and then had me. The thought of how happy they must've been when they first met roiled my stomach. The future must have looked so bright for my mom who'd grown up in this small town. Funny how things had a way of changing.

"Hi, Stu," I said as we reached the gate.

"Look at you all grown up," the old greeter gushed.

"It happens to us all," I said.

"No lie," he agreed. "I hear Crew Burke's living with you this summer."

"So it seems."

"The guy's a beast," he said as he stepped aside so we could enter.

"That's one word for him," I mumbled as I followed Gina to a spot in the host family section. I opened both of our chairs while she was busy looking for Cody on the field.

"Peyton!" someone shouted.

I spun around to find Sam on the field leaning against the fence. His uniform fit him well. The short sleeves on his red shirt showed off his impressive biceps. "Hey."

He smiled. "Glad you came."

"Whoa," I said. "We didn't get that far, buddy."

He laughed. "Did you really just say that?"

"She did," Gina interrupted, never surprised by anything that left my lips.

"Enjoy the game," he said.

"I will now that we got a good view of right field and nowhere near that reprehensible shortstop." I shivered at the thought.

"Do you even know who our shortstop is?" he asked.

I shook my head.

He laughed as he walked away and tossed the ball to one of his teammates.

"He's really cute," Gina said. "And he likes you."

"He's all right."

"Might you break your no-dating-baseball-players rule for him?" she asked.

"Nope."

Once we secured our spot on the hill, we grabbed a hot dog and a drink from the concession stand. From there, we watched a local girl sing the national anthem as the players and fans stood facing the flag in centerfield.

Gina and I returned to our chairs as the first pitch was thrown. I scanned the field for familiar faces. I spotted Sam in right field, and Gina pointed out Cody behind the plate in catcher's gear. I scoffed once I saw the shortstop.

Of course, it was Crew.

I didn't recognize the pitcher, but the announcer said that he stood at six five and attended the University of Tennessee. He struck out the first three batters, and the Sharks jogged off the field. I tried not to look at Crew—since every other fan seemed to be, but he was like a magnet drawing me in. He filled out his uniform like a major leaguer, and the ball cap pulled down to his eyes gave the impression that he was focused on nothing but the game.

At the bottom of the first inning, Cody walked up to the plate as their leadoff batter. He was introduced as attending the University of Kansas. Gina tried not to act too excited, just clapping from her chair, but I knew she was bursting to jump to her feet—especially when he hit a single to left field. The next batter attended the University of Texas and hit into a double play causing the fans around us to groan as he and Cody were called out and jogged off the field. The third batter stepped up to the plate. As soon as his name was announced, the fans roared—scratch that. The *female* fans roared. "Crew Burke from the University of Alabama."

My stomach dropped.

Gina's mouth formed an O. "He goes to your school?"

The information played through my head. So did visions of people on campus. Had we met? Was that why he was so cold toward me? Had we hooked up and I'd forgotten?

"Peyton?" Gina asked again.

"There're almost forty thousand students. I don't know everyone."

"I bet he knows you," she said.

"Why wouldn't he say anything?"

"Have you given him the chance?" she asked.

"We don't have long conversations," I said, feeling a little guilty that I hadn't mentioned our precarious sleeping arrangement to her. But it was only because I knew what she'd say. What any rational person would say. *Why?*

On the field, Crew settled into his stance in the batter's box. The pitcher released a wicked curve ball. Crew watched it without swinging, and the ump called it a strike. Crew stepped out of the batter's box, readjusted his batting gloves, and stepped back in. The pitcher wound up and released another pitch. This one was a fast ball right over the plate. Crew swung, connecting with the ball and sending it flying high and far. The fans around me leaped to their feet just in time to see it sail over the left field fence. Crew didn't celebrate like his teammates did outside the dugout. He just trotted around the bases with his head down, showing no excitement. He was all business. Once he reached home and his teammates slapped his hand one by one, I glimpsed the slightest smile on his face before he disappeared into the dugout.

"He's so hot."

I glanced to a girl around my age seated with a friend nearby.

"I heard he hooked up with Val the other night," her friend said.

"I thought he was hooking up with Steph?" she asked.

Her friend shrugged. "These guys get around."

They sure did.

When the Sharks ran out onto the field for the top of the second inning, the girls beside us cheered, and I could tell their attention was directed at Crew.

I rolled my eyes and scrolled through the feed on my phone.

"Welcome back," Janie, a girl Gina and I had grown up with at the beach, stopped beside us.

"Thanks," I said, knowing we were in for an earful.

Her eyes moved to the field. "How's Crew doing?"

"Let me guess. Another Crew fan?" I said.

"Who isn't?" she said, the awe in her voice impossible to ignore.

"The guy might be good at baseball, but he's a player," I said.

"Yeah. He's definitely not looking for anything serious," Janie agreed. "But I think the girls around here see that as a challenge. Like, who will be the one to make him commit."

"Good luck with that," Gina said, without tearing her eyes away from Cody.

"From what I hear," Janie continued, "he doesn't even do a lot of talking behind closed doors."

"Just wham-bam-thank-you-ma'am?" I said.

"Exactly," she explained. "And, he takes their phones away."

"What?" Gina asked, finally tearing her eyes off of Cody.

Janie nodded. "Weird, right?"

"Actually, it's pretty smart," I said.

They both looked to me, waiting for my rationale. "He probably doesn't want to risk any videos of him going viral, especially if he's got any shot of getting drafted."

"Makes sense," Janie agreed. "So, all these girls get left with is the memory—"

"And the crummy T-shirt," I added.

Gina and Janie laughed.

"He seriously doesn't talk?" I asked.

Janie shrugged. "From what I hear, not really."

"That's weird," Gina interjected.

"Yeah," I said, "since he has no trouble voicing his disdain for all things me."

The left fielder caught the third out, and the Sharks jogged off the field. As they did, I spotted Crew and his eyes were locked on mine, narrowing coldly. *What the hell?* Didn't he just tell me—behind closed doors—that he wasn't my enemy? Because he was sure acting like it.

CHAPTER SEVEN

I walked through the kitchen and into the living room, running my finger over the back of the sofa as I passed by it. I stopped at the sofa table that held photos of the many summers spent at the beach. I'd been so happy in the photos with my parents over the years. My father's giant smile had always made me think he was so happy with our family. His athletic arms were wrapped tightly around me in most of the photos, always making me feel so safe. So special. So loved. Tears glazed my eyes as I looked at my mother's smiles. She was so beautiful. So happy. So oblivious. Just like me.

Preventing my mind from venturing to further dark places, I climbed the stairs to the second floor. I moved past my room and went into the guest room. I didn't feel like messing with Crew tonight. What Janie said about him struck a chord with me. Him hooking up with faceless girls was the reason I despised ball players like him—and my father.

I grabbed some clean clothes, then walked into the bathroom, undressed, and showered, cleaning my skin of the humidity in the air. Once I finished, I slipped on my panties and a T-shirt, pulled my wet hair up in a messy knot on the top of my head, and climbed into bed. Sleep found me sooner than I expected.

———

"Why'd you leave before the game ended?" Crew's voice was a blur between my dreams and reality.

I stirred.

"Were you bored?" The weight of his body dipped the mattress. "You missed my second home run."

I grunted.

"Other girls would've been impressed," he said, more surprised than bragging.

"I have a face. I'm not other girls," I finally mumbled.

"That's abundantly clear."

I opened my eyes. He was on the edge of the bed taking off his sneakers.

"What happened to your hand?" I asked, noticing the bandage wrapped around the palm of his left hand.

"I had a splinter. It got infected."

"A splinter at the beach?"

He cocked his head, as if I should've understood how he got a splinter.

"*Ohhhhh*," I said, realizing *he'd* picked up the pieces of my broken Adirondack chair.

"Most people would say, 'Thank you.'"

"Why? It seems like karma to me."

He closed his eyes and shook his head, as if he couldn't figure me out.

"Why are you even in here?" I asked.

"I got used to sleeping next to you."

"It was twice," I countered.

He lifted the sheets and climbed underneath, facing me on his side. "Three times."

"I left you alone. I came in here."

"And I followed. Ball's in your court now," he said.

"It was a stupid game." I rolled away from him. "I quit."

"Didn't take you for a quitter," he said, his breath now tickling the back of my neck.

I wasn't a quitter. I was still in Cape Cod, wasn't I? "I learned something about you tonight," I said. "Despite your many wild nights here on the Cape, you don't do a lot of talking."

"Talking's overrated."

"It's such a shame that these girls are missing out on all the insightful things you add to our conversations."

He stayed silent.

"Why didn't you tell me we went to the same school?" I asked.

"What's it matter?" he asked. "It's a big school. We don't run in the same circles."

"But you knew I went there?"

"You're Marty Richmond's daughter. Word gets around."

"I'm more than Marty Richmond's daughter."

"Oh, I can see that."

That seemed too easy. "So, we've never—"

"Slept together?"

I gasped. "What? No. I was gonna say *met?*"

He laughed. "I'm just messing with you."

"It would explain what I did to piss you off so much though," I said.

"No, that was you screaming like a banshee and throwing a chair off of a balcony."

"You were screwing a girl on my balcony!"

"While you were supposed to be gone for the whole summer."

"It doesn't make it any less gross."

"Why's it gross? I certainly didn't need to force her into it."

"Oh, I could see that."

He grew silent. Had he run out of comebacks?

I considered what he said about expecting me to be gone for the summer. Maybe I had surprised them. Maybe I had appeared to them a little crazy. But *come on*. Who wants to ever walk in on that?

"Why'd you come back early, anyway?" he asked.

"It was a mistake."

"Because *I'm* here or for other reasons?"

I yawned. "Both."

Mr. Talking's Overrated finally reached his quota—or he didn't like my answer—because he said nothing else.

CHAPTER EIGHT

Persistent knocking echoed from the front door. I moved from the kitchen down the first-floor hallway to the door and pulled it open. A woman and a small girl stood hand in hand staring at me. Neither smiled. Neither looked familiar. "Can I help you?" I asked.

"We're looking for Marty Richmond," the woman said.

"Can I tell him who's here?" I asked.

"Tell him Misty from San Diego."

A pit formed in my stomach. "No last name?"

"He'll know," she assured me.

"Peyton?" a deep voice from somewhere far away called.

"Why will he know?" I asked her.

Misty's eyes cut to the little girl beside her.

"Peyton?" the deep voice repeated, trying to get me out of that hallway.

"Why will he know?" I asked, the desperation in my voice impossible to disguise.

"Peyton, wake up," Crew said, shaking me.

My eyes popped open. Sweat beaded to my hairline and

tears glazed my eyes as the auburn hues of dawn filled my room.

"Are you okay?" he asked.

I nodded, though I knew I was far from it.

"It was just a dream," he assured me.

His assurance that it was only a dream couldn't erase the memory of that day. Nothing could. Because the truth was, it wasn't just a dream. It was how it all played out last summer. But Misty wasn't the woman who'd shown up. One night it was Candy from Minnesota. Other times it was Angel from Colorado. Sometimes Vikki from Boston. Or even Santana from New York. My subconscious was telling me there were more women. But the little girl was always the same. Those haunting blue eyes belonged to my father. "I..." I choked on the word. "It was nothing."

"It didn't sound that way."

I closed my eyes; I didn't want him to see me that way.

"Do you remember what it was about?" he pried.

"No," I lied, quickly rolling off the bed and onto my feet. "I've gotta go," I said as I took off for the door.

"Wait!" he called.

But, I was already gone, feeling uncomfortable and vulnerable and nauseous. I didn't want him consoling me. I was tougher than that.

I locked myself in my bedroom and then hurried into the shower, standing in there for far longer than necessary. I felt so stupid. It was one thing for Crew to find out about my nightmares the way he had, but to try to be there for me was not something I needed from him. If Gina knew we were sleeping in the same bed, she'd say something like, 'It *seemed* like you needed him.' Or, 'It's good to need other people.' But Crew wasn't other people. He was someone who rubbed me the wrong way.

Someone who took what he wanted when he wanted it. Case in point, him tracking me down last night and sleeping in the guest room. He had to know I wasn't going to be a groupie.

I finally switched off the shower and got out, wrapping myself in a towel. Now what? All of my stuff was in the guest room. I cracked the door and checked the hallway; it was empty. My father's voice trickled upstairs from the kitchen below. I listened closely and heard Crew speaking too.

I tiptoed back to the guest room and locked myself inside. I texted with my mom and watched some videos on my phone—anything to avoid a run-in with him.

Sometime later, tires crunched over the gravel in the driveway. I climbed off my bed and moved to the window that overlooked the front yard. My father's car pulled away while my mother's Jeep remained in the driveway where it had been since I arrived.

Shuffling in the hallway drew my attention to the door. Then, a piece of paper slipped underneath.

I tiptoed to it and picked it up.

Open up

I rolled my eyes and spoke through the door. "What is it, Crew?"

"Just checking if you're all right."

"People text or DM these days."

"I'm not people."

I huffed my annoyance. "I'm fine. Why wouldn't I be?"

"You ran away this morning."

"No, I didn't. I just had better things to do," I lied.

"You don't need to be embarrassed. Everyone has bad dreams."

"I'm not embarrassed," I snapped.

"Whatever."

"We're not friends, Crew. Just leave me alone."

He was silent for a long time. And, then his footsteps retreated down the hall and my bedroom door closed.

That was the last I heard from him that day.

And I slept alone that night.

CHAPTER NINE

Gina and I spent the next day at the beach, enjoying the weather and each other's company. We didn't talk about guys or my parents. I didn't mention my nightmare, Crew coming to my room to check on me, or me sending him away. We talked about school and traveling and music. And, we laughed—which I desperately needed. Gina was someone who exuded happiness and positive energy, and, currently, that's all I needed to be surrounded by.

Once I knew that Crew would be gone for his game, I said goodbye to Gina and went back to my house. As soon as I stepped into the kitchen, I regretted it.

"I'm heading to Boston for the weekend," my father said from his spot at the sink.

I grabbed a water from the refrigerator. "And?"

"I just thought you'd want to know."

I closed the refrigerator and began to walk away. "Nope."

"Careful, Peyton," he warned.

I stopped and spun around.

"You may just get what you wish for and end up alone."

"Unlike you, I don't need other people to make me happy." I stormed off, feeling my heartbeat slamming in my chest.

Once I entered the guest room, I dropped down onto the edge of the bed with shaking hands and beads of sweat along my hairline.

Dammit.

Why did I let him get to me?

These interactions were doing a number on my mental health. I knew why my mother wanted me there, but maybe I couldn't handle it. Because the nightmare this morning, and my body's reaction right now, told me this was just the beginning.

———

Loud music outside woke me from a sound sleep. I checked my phone and it was nearing midnight. I sat up and threw my legs out from under my covers. I crept to the window and found a patio filled with people.

What the hell?

Girls and guys jumped into the pool, laughing and splashing around like they were at some Spring Break pool party.

That son of a bitch was throwing a party at *my* house.

I tugged on shorts and marched downstairs, unable to believe he'd think throwing a party was okay.

"Hey," Sam said as soon as I stepped outside.

"Why are *you* here?" I asked, my eyes taking in the thirty to forty people taking over my patio and pool.

"Hello to you too," he said.

I shook my head. "Sorry. I just meant, why is Crew throwing a party?"

"He said your dad's out of town. I kinda wish he was here so I could meet him."

I ground my teeth together. "Where's Crew?"

Sam looked around until he spotted him, then pointed toward a chair by the pool house "Oh, he's with CC."

My head whipped around, my eyes narrowing when I spotted him sitting there with a bikini-clad CC in his lap. God, could he get any more predictable?

"Hey, great party," a guy said as he passed by me.

"I wouldn't know," I clipped.

A group of guys and girls cheering around the table drew my attention. There was a guy and girl on each end of the table. One of the girls rolled a pair of dice. She and her partner dropped their heads back in frustration as their opponents bumped fists when they saw the dice.

"Strip!" someone called.

They all cheered as the girl pulled off her bikini top and the guy dropped his bathing trunks. They bolted toward the pool and jumped in.

Sam laughed. "I'm gonna get a drink. You want one?"

I shook my head, and Sam took off for one of the coolers. I looked back to where Crew was, wanting him to shut the party down. But he'd disappeared.

"Everybody in the pool!" someone yelled.

Half the party took off for the pool and jumped in.

Arms grasped me around my waist from behind. I struggled to get free, but I was pulled to the pool. I held my breath at the last second before we plunged under water. Only then, did I finally pull free and surface. I looked to the guy who'd pulled me in and shoved him. "Idiot!"

"Whoa. They said, 'Everyone in,'" he argued.

"Did I look like I wanted to go in?!"

He looked at me like I was crazy. But who pulled someone into the water who wasn't even in a bathing suit?

I climbed out of the pool and grabbed a towel from a pile on a chair. I wrapped it around me and began to move toward the back door.

"Is your dad here?"

I looked beside me to the girl in a tiny red bikini who'd asked the question. "Excuse me?"

"Your dad. Is he here?" She looked around as if she'd actually find him hanging out at a party filled with college kids.

"No."

"Too bad. For an older guy, he's so freakin' hot," she said.

My heart began to race.

"Is he into younger girls?"

Sweat beaded on my forehead. "He's married," I said, though my words sounded as if they were in a fishbowl.

"Doesn't mean he wouldn't want me," she said like she wasn't talking about my father.

My hands began to tingle. "You know what? You're probably right." I spun away from her, suddenly unable to catch my breath. It was as if an imaginary weight was pressed against my chest. I rushed inside the house, frantically reaching the kitchen sink and bracing my hands on it. I needed to catch my breath, but I was seconds away from passing out. I moved unsteadily away from the sink and to the island, pushing aside a stool and sitting on the floor beneath it. I tucked up my knees as I tried to even my breathing, but my chest tightening around my racing heart prevented me from focusing.

Breathe, Peyton. Just breathe.

"Peyton?" Crew called.

I opened my mouth to respond, but the words just wouldn't come out. My head began to swim. I focused on my breathing. *In and out. In and out.*

Crew's footsteps padded upstairs. Doors opened and closed. His footsteps padded back downstairs and moved closer until his legs were in front of me. He crouched down and found me under the island. "What are you doing down there?"

I shook my head, unable to verbalize what was happening.

His eyes widened. "What's wrong?"

I shook my head, the words still stuck inside of me.

"Jesus Christ, Peyton." He kneeled in front of me and grasped my hands. I couldn't even feel his hands as mine had become numb. "You're having a panic attack. Just breathe."

I closed my eyes and focused on breathing.

"Has this happened before?"

I nodded.

"Okay, well just focus on your breathing. It will pass. You're safe. I'm here with you. I'm not going anywhere," he assured me.

In the past, if I just focused on my breathing it would eventually even out. But this time, the weight on my chest was suffocating.

We sat like that for a long time. The sounds of laughter and splashing outside began to dissipate. And, with time, my heartbeat began to slow.

"How often does this happen?" he asked.

"It depends."

"On what?"

"What triggers it."

He didn't respond, and I assumed he was trying to figure out what had done it.

If I had to guess, it was the combination of my nightmare, the run-in with my father, and that girl sounding very much like a desperate groupie who preyed on players.

"My mom gets them too," Crew admitted.

"What causes hers?"

He shrugged. "Life."

I considered what my life would be like if the episodes didn't pass and happened anytime I got stressed or overwhelmed. I wouldn't be able to handle that.

"I should've asked if I could invite some people over," he said.

"It's your house too."

"Yeah, but..."

"You wanted to piss me off?"

He shrugged, but I knew it was the truth.

"I'm sorry I was a bitch yesterday." I tucked a wet clump of hair behind my ear noticing the numbness in my hand had almost worn off.

"I'm sure you had a good reason."

I pushed myself to my knees. "People are probably looking for you."

"I don't care."

I moved out from under the island and stood up. My legs were jelly, but I was pretty sure I could make it upstairs without an issue.

Crew stood up beside me. "Are you good?"

"Yeah. I'm just gonna head upstairs."

"You want some help?"

I shook my head. "I'm fine."

His lips pulled to the side, and I could tell he was debating whether or not to leave me alone.

"I'm *fine*," I assured him. "It wasn't the first and it certainly won't be the last. I've gotta learn to deal." I didn't wait for him to respond. I left him and went upstairs to the guest room. I pulled off the wet clothes and slipped on some dry ones. I climbed under the covers, trying to forget this day ever happened.

"Everyone out!" Crew shouted outside. "Party's over."

People groaned and footsteps scampered around. Car engines started in the front yard. And, before long, all I could hear were the ocean waves crashing and Crew moving patio furniture back to where it belonged.

Sometime after I'd fallen asleep, I heard the door open and footsteps neared my bed. I wanted to tell him to stop. But as he lifted the sheets and slipped into the bed behind me, I said nothing.

"Are you okay?" Crew whispered.

"I'm not a delicate flower you need to look after," I said, a little harsher than I should've.

"I never said you were."

Twice he'd come to my rescue. Twice he'd seen me weak. I needed to gain my footing again. That's why all of this was happening in the first place. Everything felt so out of my control. My world was spiraling and nothing I did or said seemed to have the ability to stop it.

"My mom takes medication for hers," he said.

"I don't need it."

"Well, if you're ever alone and—"

"I said, 'I don't need it.'"

A long stretch of silence passed, and I hoped he was done talking for the night. My mind was mush, and my body was spent.

"Sam was looking for you," he said.

"Did you tell him..."

"I said you went to bed," he assured me.

I closed my eyes and exhaled. At least he wasn't telling everyone my business.

"I think he was bummed you didn't show up to the game," he continued.

"I'm sure he didn't care."

"Oh, come on. You've gotta see that the guy likes you."

"We're friends," I assured him.

"*Right.*"

Normally, I'd argue, but all my energy had been depleted from the panic attack. "He knows I don't date baseball players."

"If you say so."

He didn't believe me? "If I didn't know any better, I'd think you were jealous."

"Maybe I am," he said.

I rolled my eyes. Players didn't get jealous. Players made people jealous. And then they stomped on their hearts.

"I missed sleeping next to you last night," he continued.

"Oh, that was a good one. I can see how groupies would fall for your lines."

"It wasn't a line," Crew assured me.

"Uh huh," I said.

He didn't respond. Neither did I. We were getting good at leaving the other with something to think about. I may have thought about it...until I fell asleep.

CHAPTER TEN

Sunlight poured through the windows in the guest room. A slight headache pulsed in my temples.

"Morning."

I squinted as I looked to my left.

Crew lay on his back beside me with his eyes closed.

"Why are you still here?" I asked.

His head fell to the side, and he looked at me with sleepy eyes. "I'm not used to getting kicked out of someone's bed."

"That's because you're usually invited."

"Yet here I am," he said. "Why do you think that is?"

"You enjoy annoying me?" I said, rolling away from him. I felt the bed shift with his weight, so I glanced over my shoulder.

He sat perched on the edge of the bed. "You hungry?"

"What?" I asked.

He glanced over his shoulder at me. "Let's get some breakfast."

"Why?"

"Why not?"

"That doesn't sound like a good idea."

"Why can't two people who sleep in the same bed share a meal?"

"Why should they?" I countered.

"Because I'm hungry. And, there is nothing wrong with us hanging out."

At the moment, my stomach rumbled. There was no way that he hadn't heard it because his lips twitched. "Only because I'm starving am I even considering it."

"Stop being so tough and have breakfast with me."

"You're paying."

A small smile slipped across his lips. "Of course."

———

"Five-hundred and thirty-six," I said before taking a bite of my vegetable omelet.

Crew stared down at his phone from the opposite side of the booth. "That's *nuts*. Okay. One more. Jeter?"

"Two-hundred and sixty," I said without even thinking about it.

"Shut up," Crew said, amazed that I knew the number of lifetime home runs certain baseball players had off the top of my head.

"I told you I knew."

He shook his head and placed his phone down on the table. "I've never met a girl who knew so much about baseball."

"What do you think dinnertime talks were like when he was home? You'd think he'd need a break from it during the off-season, but nope."

"What *was* it like growing up with him?"

"I think you're forgetting he was only home for a four-month stretch each year. But when he was home, I was his whole world. I'd follow him around everywhere. People called me his shadow. God, I thought he was larger than life. Then I learned he wasn't."

"No?"

I shrugged. "Long story."

He glanced around the empty café. "I've got nowhere to be."

"I'm not about to unload my sob story on a guy I hated up until a few minutes ago."

"So, let me get this straight. You don't hate me anymore?"

I bit back a smile. "I'm starting to be able to stomach you."

He laughed. "Stomach me? Gee, I'm glad to hear you can stomach me."

The bell on the door jingled. Crew quickly pulled the brim of his hat down lower until it was nearly covering his eyes.

I glanced over my shoulder expecting to see one of his hook-ups. But two guys in Sharks ball caps walked toward us.

"Hey, Burke," one of them said.

Crew glanced up as if he hadn't noticed them enter. "What's up, Pryor? DePetrillo?"

Pryor, the jerk who'd pulled me in the pool, looked to me and stifled a smile. "Never wear a white T-shirt to a pool party."

My jaw clenched. "Seriously?"

Crew reached across the table and placed his hand on my arm. "Don't."

Who did he think he was telling me not to talk?

"What time you heading to the field?" DePetrillo interjected.

"We've got the autograph thing first," Crew said as he removed his hand from my arm. "So, I'll probably get there at three."

They both groaned.

"Get used to it if you think you're going to the big leagues," Crew said.

"See you later," Pryor said heading to a booth away from ours.

"I hope not," I mumbled.

Once they were gone, Crew looked to me. "Thank you."

"For what?"

"For not doing that thing you do."

My brows shot up. "That thing I do?"

"Yeah. The thing where you're ready to fight anyone who looks at you the wrong way."

"I don't do that," I challenged.

"You do that more than any person I've ever met."

I rolled my eyes.

"Not everyone hates you, Peyton. Not everyone is trying to wrong you. Not everyone deserves your bad attitude."

"There is nothing bad about my attitude," I said, though I didn't even believe my own words.

He took a bite of his pancakes instead of bothering to debate it.

"So, autographs tonight?" I said, trying to swing the conversation back to him since I knew he gave very little up without prompting.

"Yup."

"You know it makes the little kids' nights when you guys do that," I said, having been one of those kids before.

His lips twitched. "With great power comes great responsibility."

"I'm serious."

"I am too. I take it seriously. I know what I say to them in that brief time means something."

I took another bite of my omelet.

"And one day, when I'm in the majors, they'll sell that autograph for a lot of money."

I smiled. "Did you know the percentage of Cape League players drafted to the pros is under thirty-five percent?"

"Better than zero," he said.

I liked his optimism. "Do you think you'll make it?"

"Do you?"

My lips twisted in contemplation. "I hope not."

His head shot back. "Why not?"

"Because it does bad things to people."

He tilted his head, his eyes moving over my features. "I'm not other people. I make my own decisions."

"You say that now. Then, fame and money happen."

"When are you gonna tell me what happened?"

"When are you gonna stop asking?" I clipped.

He dragged his napkin across his lips. "Right now." He reached into his pocket and tossed forty dollars onto the table.

"I changed my mind about you paying," I said, digging into my own pocket and pulling out my credit card.

He reached across the table and rested his hand on my arm like he'd done before. I tried to ignore the little ripples that erupted beneath his touch. "I'm paying."

"This isn't a date," I said.

"Oh, that is abundantly clear. You don't date ball players," he said.

"I'm glad you've been paying attention."

His eyes locked on mine. "It's hard not to."

My eyes narrowed. Was that an insult or his attempt at flirting?

He pushed himself to his feet and I followed, not about to argue over a check. Once we stepped outside, we began to walk back toward the house, but I stopped. "You head back. I'm gonna stop by some of the shops."

His brows knitted together. "What could the girl who has everything possibly need to buy?"

"I definitely don't have everything."

He buried his hands in his pockets and moved toward me. "Liar."

I shook my head, the list of things I wanted but couldn't have was at the forefront of my brain: Love. Trust. Loyalty.

"You coming to the game tonight?" he asked.

"Probably not."

"Well, for what it's worth, I wouldn't hate it if you showed up."

"Why's that? Don't you have a big enough cheering section?"

He laughed. "It can never be big enough."

I groaned. "See?"

"What?"

"That arrogance—"

"Oh, come on. You left that one wide open for me."

"For you to what?"

"I *do* have a cheering section. It comes with the territory."

"You're right. That's why I hate all of you." I spun away from him and headed toward the shops.

"Lucky for you," he shouted after me. "I don't hate you."

He didn't follow me which was good because I needed

time away from him. Though, it would've been easier if his scent didn't cling to me. I guess that happened when you slept beside someone.

I strolled through a hat shop, then a portrait shop, before walking around a jewelry shop. I needed a shell necklace—the kind you could only find by the beach. I bought a new one every summer, wearing it until it broke at some point during the year, just in time to get a new one.

"That's pretty," the woman behind the counter said as I pulled a white and coral shelled necklace off the display hanger.

"It is pretty," I agreed as I held it up to my neck in the counter mirror.

"Where are you visiting us from?" the woman asked.

"I live here every summer," I explained. "But I go to school in Alabama."

"Well, I think you need a keepsake from the Cape when you go back to Alabama."

"I'll take this one."

"Pretty in pink," she mused.

I put the necklace on while she rang me up, knowing I'd keep it on until it broke.

"Peyton!" Gina called as I stepped out of the shop.

"Hey," I said as she approached me.

"Whatcha doing?"

I ran my fingers gently over the small shells around my neck. "Just needed a new necklace."

"It's so pretty. It reminds me of the one we got when we were like ten. Remember we bought the same one?"

I nodded.

"Soooo," she began, "since when do you throw parties and not invite me?"

I rolled my eyes. "That was all Crew."

"Did you actually hang with baseball players?"

I shook my head. "I only went outside to shut the party down."

"Next time, call me. Cody and I would've come over."

"Oh, there better not be a next time."

She laughed. "You wanna drive with me to the game tonight?"

"I think one game was enough for me."

"Come on," she pleaded. "I can't go alone."

"Of course you can," I assured her.

"There are so many girls hanging around just trying to catch the eye of one of the guys. I can't fight them off all by myself."

My stomach turned at the thought of girls trying to get with a player. Didn't these girls realize many of the guys had serious relationships back home? Did they even care? "Gold digging whores."

"Exactly. They want to latch onto them for what they might become."

"Well, lucky for you, your family's loaded. Cody has to know you're not in it for the money."

She laughed. "You think so?"

"Besides that, look at you," I said, my eyes drifting over her flowy peach sundress. "You wouldn't be caught dead in a ball cap and cutoffs."

Her brows dipped. "What does that have to do with anything?"

"Well, it means you're not trying to be anyone but yourself."

"You think?"

"I know."

"So, does that mean you'll go with me?" she asked.

"No."

"*Peyton*," she whined.

"*Gina*," I teased.

"I'll owe you."

"I *will* make you pay up."

"Deal."

Dammit. I was going to another stupid baseball game.

CHAPTER ELEVEN

s soon as Gina and I made our way through the entrance, I spotted the big event tent and heard loud music coming from it. Kids with their parents rushed by us in order to get to it.

"I wonder what's going on over there," Gina said.

"Cody didn't tell you? The guys are signing autographs before the game."

"How do you know?"

"Crew told me."

"Crew?" She stopped, eyeing me curiously. "Are you guys talking now?"

I shrugged.

"Why is it you tell me nothing?"

"Nothing to tell," I said as we headed toward the tent. Three long tables were set up, and the baseball players sat on one side while the little kids stopped to visit each player, getting autographs on photos, balls, or bats while their parents took photos.

"Look how good he is with kids," Gina gushed.

I knew she meant Cody, but my eyes were focused on

Crew, who sat at the very end of the line of players. Kid after kid approached him, and, to my surprise, he took his time speaking to each of them. His eyes shifted between the kid and whatever he was signing for them with a genuine smile on his face. The mothers always stood nearby; their smiles were just as wide as their kids'.

I wasn't blind.

I understood the charm. Crew was good-looking, athletic, and his lines were convincing. But he was no different than the others. He proved it with the number of girls I'd seen him with in the short time I'd been back. He'd make them fall for him. Then, he'd find another one in some other town. It was inevitable.

As if he could sense me staring across the tent, his eyes lifted to mine and a slow smile spread across his face. Of course, he'd think I was there for him. So, instead of letting him think he was right, I raised my middle finger to my cheek and scratched.

He laughed before returning his attention to the kid in front of him, smiling at him like whatever he was saying was the most important thing he'd heard all day.

"Let's go get a spot," I said to Gina.

"You go. I wanna watch Cody interact with the kids some more. It's so adorable."

"Suit yourself." I turned and made my way over to the first base line.

Other families greeted me as I took a spot on the grass. I stared out at the field as the groundkeeper raked the dirt around home plate, getting lost in my thoughts.

I wondered how many sides there were to Crew. The athlete. The womanizer. The hero to little kids. The caretaker. I pulled out my phone, wondering why it took me so long to stalk his socials. Surprisingly, he didn't have any, so I searched up his name. Baseball photos appeared first. Some were high school photos while many were college photos. He hadn't changed too much over the years. His jawline had definitely become more defined and chiseled and muscles had filled out his short-sleeved jersey. I continued to scroll and stumbled upon photos of him at parties with girls and teammates clearly pulled from social media. A tinge of jealousy swirled inside me.

"Whatcha doing?"

I flipped off my phone and looked up to find Sam standing there. "Hey."

"Glad you made it to another game," he said. "Figured you were done for the season."

"Yet, here I am."

"Hoping to see me?" he asked.

I laughed.

"Sorry I didn't get to say goodbye last night," he said.

"Yeah, sorry. I got so tired all of a sudden."

"No worries. As long as you were okay."

"Hey, I bet you made some kid's day today," I said, swiftly changing the subject.

He smiled. "Yeah. They love meeting us."

"I still have all of my autographs from when I was a kid," I said.

"Yeah?"

I nodded. "Never missed a game."

"You want my autograph?" he asked.

"Will it be worth something someday?"

"Let's hope so."

Someone called Sam's name, and he turned to see who it was. He looked back to me. "I gotta go get changed. You staying for the whole game?"

I shrugged. "If I don't get bored."

He laughed before disappearing toward the field house.

I switched my phone back on and continued my search. I read through some articles about Crew's stats and the many awards he'd won. He was on a full ride to Alabama for baseball.

"Well, that was fun," Gina said as she approached holding a blanket.

"Did you clean up the drool?" I asked as she spread out the blanket beside me.

"Shut up. It was adorable," she said as she sat down on the blanket. "I couldn't help but watch."

I scooted onto the blanket.

"Did you know the sponsorship banquet's tomorrow night?" she asked.

"Why would I know that? Or care?"

"Because, besides the Fourth of July which you missed, you know it's the biggest event of the summer and all the host families go."

"Lucky for you, your family didn't host this year," I said.

"Yes, but Cody invited me," she countered.

"Exciting," I said, trying to sound excited for her.

"Are you going with your—"

"Absolutely not."

"Well, then I have good news. Cody said I could bring you. You can sit with us and his host family."

"No, thanks."

"*Please.*"

"You don't need me there," I assured her.

"Of course I do. If you don't recall, there were many summers that I followed you around on your crazy adventures, most of them involving cute boys. I never said no. I just acted as your loyal wingman. Now, I finally have something going well for me, and you want to deny me this happiness?"

I rolled onto my back. "*Ohmigod*. Could you be any more dramatic?"

"Absolutely," she said.

I laughed, knowing she was right. Summer after summer I dragged her on missions to find cute boys, and she never *once* let me down.

"What else are you gonna be doing?" she persisted.

"Painting my nails. Scrolling social media. Sleeping."

"*Peyton?*"

"Fine."

"Fine?" she asked.

I pushed myself back up. "I'll go to the ridiculous banquet."

"You will?"

"Don't make me say it again."

She squealed. "Thank you! We're gonna have so much fun."

"Speak for yourself," I said, very aware the whole night was gonna suck.

"Let's go shopping for dresses," she said, like it was the most fun thing we could do together.

"Let's," I said, my tone telling her just how unappealing it sounded.

"Don't worry. You'll be in our wedding," she said.

My brows shot up. "What?"

"When all of this works out, and Cody and I decide to get married, I want you to be my maid of honor."

"Getting a little ahead of ourselves, aren't we, crazy girl?" I asked.

"I'm manifesting it," she explained. "I'm putting it out in the universe to make it happen."

"Uh-huh."

"And, because of your help, I know it will."

"I know what you're doing," I assured her.

"What am I doing?"

"You're making it so I can't back out, even if I want to."

She pressed her hand to her chest. "Me?"

I swatted her hand away from her chest. "Yes, you conniving little bitch."

She laughed. "You know, you're the only one I'd ever let call me that?"

"I love ya, bitch."

———

Somewhere in the middle of the night I felt a slight tugging around my neck. I swatted at it and heard soft laughter in the darkness. It was Crew lying beside me, and I realized he was toying with the shells on my necklace.

"What time is it?" I muttered.

"Three a.m."

"Did you just get in?"

"I think so," he said, a slight slur to his words.

"Wild night?"

He chuckled. "How could it be? You weren't there."

I didn't respond, but it didn't matter. He continued playing with the shells around my neck. "I like your necklace..."

"Yeah?"

"It's pretty like you."

I groaned. "How much did you drink tonight?"

"How'd you know I had some drinks?"

"Because not only are you slurring, you're talking crazy."

"No, I'm not. Your necklace is pretty," he said. "And so are you."

I tried not to smile.

"Pretty, powerful, proud...Peyton is," Crew said. "See? I'm a poet too."

"Drunk is what you are."

"Are you going to school to be a poet?' he asked.

"That's not a real thing. I'm going to be a journalist."

"Be a sports journalist so you can write about me," he said.

"You know, you won't get to the pros by going out and getting wasted."

"I can get wasted if I wanna. We've got a night off tomorrow."

"Yeah, I heard. You've got the big banquet."

"You gonna be there?" he asked.

"Why?"

He finally released my necklace and fell onto his back. "So I can see you," he mumbled before the soft purr of sleep replaced his words.

CHAPTER TWELVE

I entered Gina's room, carrying my dress by the hanger. It had taken three hours for her to pick out her dress this morning and five minutes for me—after I'd woken up alone in bed. I wondered if Crew disappeared so early because he was embarrassed by what he'd said last night. Or, if he even remembered.

"Hey," Gina said from her vanity, looking so excited to be going to the banquet.

"Hey," I said.

"I can't wait to see you in your dress again," she said. "You look so beautiful in it."

I balked. "Too bad I've got no one to impress."

"Are you kidding? Do you know how many of Cody's teammates want to tame the angry Peyton?"

I cocked my head. "What?"

"Yeah. Cody told me."

"They were talking about me?" I asked, unable to believe my ears. Was I the laughing stock of the team? Had they taken wagers on who could get with me? No. Fucking. Way.

"What's wrong?" Gina asked, noting the vacant look on my face.

I shook my head as my heart drummed faster and a cold chill rushed over my body. "Nothing."

She smiled and I could see she had no idea what she'd done by telling me that.

"I'll be right back," I said as I rushed out of her room and into the bathroom. I closed the door, and with my back to it, I slipped down to the floor.

Had I really been a bet?

Was that why Crew paid for breakfast? Why he was all *you're as pretty as your necklace?*

I would not cry.

I would not give into the overwhelming feeling of dread taking over my body. I would not give in to the feeling of my world being out of my control.

I was in control.

I pulled in a deep breath, releasing it slowly despite the imaginary weight pressing against my chest. I was stronger than this.

Gina knocked on the door. "Peyton? Are you all right?"

"I just need a minute."

"Did I say something to upset you?" she asked.

"No," I lied. "I just need a few more minutes."

An hour later, I'd battled the panic attack and won. My fitted navy dress stopped midthigh and my nude heels made me inches taller. My makeup was flawless and contoured in all the right places. Gina had curled my hair into beachy waves and I was ready to get this night over with.

I took in Gina in her red dress, whistling a long-drawn-out whistle. "Cody is going to fall over when he sees you."

"And, every guy in that banquet hall is gonna fall over when they see you," she assured me.

There was only one player I hoped fell over. It'd be easier to stomp on him that way. "Let's do this."

Our Uber drove us to the beachside banquet hall in the next town. My heartbeat began to hasten as the driver stopped in front of the massive one-story structure. I opened the car door and stepped out. Gina followed me as we made our way to the entrance. A couple ball players in suits and ties opened the door, their eyes drifting over us in quiet approval. Normally, I would have spewed a snarky comment, but I wasn't about to give them anything else to talk about.

We snaked our way through the crowded lobby, past the gift basket raffle. Two ball players sat behind the table, their eyes following us as we passed by without stopping to buy tickets. We headed toward the music and into the large banquet hall. The room was filled with at least twenty large round tables—ten on either side of the dance floor.

Heads turned when we entered. I spotted Crew talking to a teammate until he noticed me. His eyes widened and a slow smile crept across his lips.

I averted my gaze and sought out Sam. He too was looking my way.

"You go find Cody. I'm gonna say hi to Sam," I said to Gina before marching over to Sam. His smile grew as I moved toward him, clearly surprised I was heading in his direction.

"Wow," he said, his eyes moving over my dress.

I grabbed his hand. "Can we talk?"

His eyes shot to my hand in his. "Sure."

I pulled him away from the room toward a door that led to the beach patio. He came willingly. Once we were outside, I stopped and turned to face him. "I need you to be honest with me."

"O-kay," he said, confused by the urgency in my tone.

"Does the team have a bet going about me?"

His features stilled. "Bet?"

"Is there a bet about who can tame me?" I asked with a small quiver to my voice now that I was actually saying it aloud.

"It's not like that," he said.

"What's it like?" I asked.

"Peyton?"

I turned at the sound of my name.

Crew stood there with his hands in the pockets of his gray suit pants. "Are you okay?"

A harsh, humorless laugh burned in my throat. "Define okay."

Sam scooted around me and escaped toward the door.

"Where are you going?" I called to Sam.

"Find me later," he said before disappearing inside.

The waves crashed in the distance as the sound of muffled music trickled outside to the patio where Crew and I stood alone. In the near darkness, his light blue eyes were accentuated by his blue tie.

"What do you want?" I asked.

His head hitched back. "I saw you take off with Sam. I wanted to be sure you were okay."

"Since when do you care?"

"What?"

"You heard me. Since when do you care about anything that happens to me?"

"What the hell's going on with you? Did you have another panic attack?"

I scoffed. "You would throw that in my face."

"Throw *what* in your face?" he asked incredulously.

"The fact that you know I have panic attacks," I said. "Was it all a ploy?"

"I'm not following."

"A ploy, Crew! A ploy to tame angry Peyton."

Just like Sam's face moments before, his face faltered.

"Yeah," I said, "I know about the bet."

"There's no bet."

"Bullshit," I challenged.

"I swear. Some of the guys were talking shit because that's what guys do. And they were wondering which one of us could tame the angry...you. No money was exchanged. It was just for laughs."

"Oh, so it's funny?"

"No, it's not funny," he said, his eyes lowering to his shoes.

"What's the winner get?" I asked.

His eyes shot up. "There's no winner. It was just guys talking."

"I don't believe you."

He threw his hands out to his sides. "Well, I can't help you with that. You're the one with trust issues. Not me."

I grabbed a nearby drink that someone had left and tossed the contents in his face. "You're an asshole."

He gave a sigh of resignation, then dragged both hands over his face to wipe the liquid from it. "I'm telling you the truth. You can choose to believe it or not. But I'm not the guy you've created in your mind. I'm not gonna let you down or do something shady behind your back. But you believe I am, so there's really nothing I can do to change that." He turned away from me and walked back inside.

I stood alone with the empty glass in my hand and the ocean breeze whipping my hair around my face.

Was he right?

Did I create things in my head?

I believed he was a jerk, so I was gonna do everything in my power to keep that notion going—whether it was the truth or not.

"Here you are!" Gina said as she stepped outside. "Why are you all alone out here?"

I shook my head as I placed the empty glass back down. "I'm just getting used to the way my life is gonna be. Always alone."

She walked over and wrapped her arm around my shoulders. "Stop it. You're gonna meet someone. It just won't be a baseball player since we all know how you feel about them. Come on. Dinner's about to be served. We're sitting with the Delaney's, and we're far away from your father and Crew."

We ate pasta dinner and the conversation flowed freely between Cody, his host family, and Gina. I was seated next to the Delaney's eight-year-old son Rory who kept talking to me, which was a blessing since I didn't have to make small talk with the adults while reeling from my interaction with Crew.

Cody's arm was draped around the back of Gina's chair, and she lit up whenever he leaned in and whispered into her ear. I hoped he didn't break her heart. I hoped he was who he seemed to be.

After the ice cream dessert was served, the dinner music turned off and the coaching staff took to the stage to show their appreciation for the team sponsors. They finished their portion of the night by giving out team awards. Cody won for best sportsmanship. Our table stood and applauded as he made his way up to the stage to accept his award.

We sat down when he stepped up to the podium and stared down at the sportsmanship plaque in his hand.

"Thanks so much for this amazing award," he began. "All I've ever wanted was to be a baseball player. I never take my job lightly, but I also want to lift up the other players around me. Being a good teammate is something I always strive to be, and I appreciate that Coach Mike and his entire staff recognize that. It's been an honor playing in the Cape League for the Sharks. Thanks to the coaches, my teammates, and to all the fans, especially my awesome host family the Delaney's, and my biggest fan Gina. I'm so glad I met you."

Gina's smile couldn't get any wider while she clapped for Cody as he stepped down from the stage. When he reached our table, he showed off his plaque before sitting back down. He turned to Gina who unexpectedly grabbed his cheeks and planted a long kiss to his lips.

"Our final award of the night is for this year's MVP," Coach Mike announced from the podium. "This player shows a combination of quiet intensity and relentless determination when he plays. He may not be the loudest player on the bench, but he's also not one to celebrate his own successes with bat flips and elaborate trots around the bases. He shows what it means to lead by example. This year's MVP is Crew Burke."

The room broke into applause. I turned in my seat to see Crew stand from his table. He fist-bumped my father before he walked to the stage. I couldn't help notice the wet spot on his jacket from the drink I'd thrown in his face. I guess he should've considered himself fortunate that I hadn't thrown a bowl pasta.

On the stage, Crew accepted the MVP award from his coach. He stepped up to the podium as he stared at the award in his hands. "Thank you to Coach Mike and the rest of the Sharks coaching staff for this honor." His eyes lifted and he scanned the room. "But it feels wrong to accept an award that says I'm the most valuable player because I feel like every player on the field contributes and is essential to the team's success. So, I'll just accept this award on behalf of the rest of my team. Let's go bring home the championship, boys."

His teammates all stood from their spots at their respective tables and cheered. The rest of the room followed, applauding Crew as he made his way back to his table.

Was he the selfless guy he claimed to be in his speech? Did I have him all wrong?

With the speeches over, the DJ began playing dance music. Cody stood and held out his hand to Gina who took it eagerly. They walked out to the dance floor and began to sway to the music, despite it being a fast song. I'd never seen her this happy. Maybe she *had* manifested her happily ever after.

Rory looked over at me. "Wanna dance?"

I laughed. "Dance?"

He nodded.

"Sure." I pushed myself to my feet and followed him to the dance floor. He weaved us around couples dancing until he stopped in a spot in the very center. I grabbed his small hands and moved us from side to side.

"Spin me!" he said.

I lifted one of our joined hands and twirled him around and around.

"I'm getting dizzy!" he cried.

"Then slow down," I laughed as he tried to stand still, but his dizziness made him walk sideways.

"Are you okay?" I asked as the song changed to a slow one.

"*Yesssss,*" he said, sidestepping and trying to keep his balance.

"Hey, buddy."

Rory and I both turned to find Crew standing near us on the dance floor. He had taken off his suit jacket and the sleeves of his white button-down shirt were rolled up and his blue tie was loosened.

"Mind if I dance with Peyton?" he asked him.

My heartrate hastened. Why did he want to dance with me? Hadn't we said all that needed to be said outside?

"Sure," Rory said. "She was making me too dizzy anyways."

"*Hey,*" I admonished. "You wanted me to spin you."

He shrugged before running off and leaving Crew and me in the center of the dance floor.

Crew reached for my hips, but I stepped back. He cocked his head. "Are you really gonna do this right now?"

"Do what?"

He glanced around the room, probably worried that people were watching our interaction.

"Feel free to find one of your adoring fans to dance with," I said.

"I don't want a fan." He stepped forward and slipped his hands around my hips. "I want you."

I don't know if it was the way he said he wanted me, or because I was causing a slight scene resisting a dance with the MVP, but I slipped my arms over his shoulders and he pulled me against his chest. Since I was wearing heels, I was just up to his shoulder, so it made it easy for me to not look into his eyes as he swayed us slowly to the music.

"You look beautiful," he whispered in my ear, his breath tickling my lobe.

I said nothing, angry that I'd given in so easily.

"I would've told you that before if you weren't so hell bent on being mad at me."

I was silent as the music echoed through the room.

"This is the longest you've gone without talking," he acknowledged. "I didn't think it was possible."

"I hate you."

"No, you don't."

We danced in silence. I tried not to focus on the gentle way his hands rested on my lower back or the scent of his cologne working its way into my senses. And forget his rock-hard chest pressed to mine. I would *not* focus on that.

The song ended and another slow one began. I tried to step back, but he held onto me tightly, stopping me from leaving. "I have a proposition for you," he finally said.

I didn't respond.

"Let's start over. I think we need a clean slate."

I pulled back so I could see his eyes. "Is this part of the bet?"

"There's *no* bet," he assured me.

I shrugged, not sure if I completely believed that.

"I'm Crew and I play baseball."

"I hate baseball players."

He chuckled. "O-kay...so...I'm Crew and I sleep next to the prettiest girl in the banquet hall."

I rolled my eyes, unsusceptible to his lines.

"Your turn," he said.

"This is stupid."

"You're the one who threw a drink in my face, but here I am. So, humor me."

Was I really gonna play along with his ridiculous game?

I exhaled. "I'm Peyton and I..." Strangely, I didn't know what else to say. Who was I? I was certainly angry. And heartbroken. And a baseball player hater. But this year had been a blur of emotions—especially sadness. I didn't even know what made me happy anymore.

"I have beautiful green eyes," Crew finished for me.

"I'm more than pretty green eyes."

He laughed.

"I love the beach," I said, pleased with myself for coming up with something.

A smile tugged at the corners of his lips. "It's good to meet you, Peyton who loves the beach. I think we're gonna be great friends."

I rolled my eyes again. "You're so stupid."

"Oh, you don't want to be my friend?"

"Girls and guys can never just be friends," I said.

"Definitely not if they're sleeping in the same bed."

"Then stop sleeping in my bed."

"You first."

"Why must you challenge me?" I asked.

"Is that what I do?"

"Oh, no. You mainly piss me off."

He laughed, and his whole face lit up.

The song ended and a fast song began. Crew released his hold on me, so I dropped my arms from his shoulders and stepped back. He ticked his head toward the door. "Walk with me."

"Why?"

"Because, like I told you last night, I wanted to see you here tonight."

CHAPTER THIRTEEN

I pulled in a breath, trying not to be so contrary, and followed Crew off the dance floor and out the back door. A few people lingered on the patio as he led me out onto the beach. I stopped, slipping off my heels and kicking them to the side where no one would step on them. Crew did the same before we walked down toward the water. "Wanna sit or keep walking?"

"It's up to you," I said. "You're the one who wanted to leave."

"Didn't you?" he challenged.

"Obviously. I hate this stuff."

"Then why'd you come?"

I walked on the wet sand along the shoreline trying to avoid the water. "Gina asked me to."

"So, let me get this straight. If Gina asks you for something, you do it?"

"Pretty much."

"Why?"

"Because I trust her wholeheartedly."

"Must be nice to have someone like that," he said. "Is she the only one?"

I considered his question as the waves crashed at our feet. "Besides my mom, yes."

"I'm here too," he offered.

I balked. "Not for long."

"We go to the same school."

I stopped and looked at him. "You said it yourself. We don't run in the same circles."

"We could," he said.

"Right."

"Oh, I'm sorry. Are you more of a football groupie?"

I groaned and continued walking.

"What?" he asked, keeping pace with me.

"Don't ever call me a groupie. I'm a football *fan*," I said with the emphasis on fan.

"Football players suck."

"Seren Grayson's one of my friends."

"Oh, so you're crushing on the quarterback," he said.

"We're just friends," I assured him.

"You said it yourself. Guys and girls can't just be friends."

"Well, we are. He has a girlfriend. And I respect that."

"Well, maybe when we get back, you can hang with me and some of my friends. You might like them."

"Why would you want me around? We can't get along for more than a few minutes at a time."

He stepped in front of me, his blue eyes settling on mine. "I don't want to fight with you."

"What do you want?"

"I want you to fucking trust me."

"Why?"

"Because I think I've earned it."

I stayed silent, unsure why it was so important to him.

"I get that your trust issues have something to do with your dad," he prompted.

I gnawed on my bottom lip, reluctant to admit it.

"I'm thinking he did something unforgivable." He stared into my eyes, looking for confirmation. "Did he cheat?"

I nodded.

He winced. "Recently?"

"I found out last summer when the woman showed up at our beach house with his daughter."

Crew's eyes widened. "Je-sus. I didn't see that one coming."

"You're not the only one. It was like a punch to the gut."

"I'd say."

"He claimed not to know she had a kid, but how can we believe anything he says now?"

"Have you met the kid?" he asked.

"Just that day, but I assure you, it wasn't a pleasant meeting," I said, the recollections of that day never far from my mind.

"Does he have anything to do with her now?" he asked.

I shrugged. "As far as I know, he pretends she doesn't exist. But then again, he's like a stranger to me. So I have no idea what he does when no one's around."

"Seems like the kid's as innocent as you in this mess," Crew observed, though he couldn't possibly understand what it felt like to learn your perfect life wasn't perfect at all.

I shrugged.

"Your hate toward baseball players finally makes sense," he said. "But we're not all like that."

"Are you forgetting I've seen you in action?" I asked.

"I'm single. I can have fun," he countered.

"And have fun you do."

He cocked his head, unamused by my commentary. "If I had a girlfriend, I'd be faithful."

"Have you ever had a serious girlfriend?"

"No."

"Well, just having a girlfriend doesn't mean the temptation isn't there. You could easily stray. Groupies can be persuasive."

He shook his head. "I'm not that guy."

"I didn't think my dad was that guy either. He was the man I trusted most in this world. And look how that turned out. I won't let that happen to me." I looked out at the crashing waves, suddenly feeling way too vulnerable.

"Did your panic attacks start after you found out about your dad?"

"That day."

"Is that why you went away this summer? So you didn't have to come back here?" he asked.

I glanced to him. "Am I that transparent?"

He shook his head. "I think you're that smart."

"You're such a liar."

He smiled, knowing I thought everything out of his mouth was a line. "Seriously though, why don't you go with your mom? She's in Alabama, right?"

I nodded. "She wanted me and my father to work things out."

"Is that what *you* want?"

"Hell no."

"Then why not go now?"

Did I tell him that I was beginning to believe that him sleeping in my bed was one of the only things keeping the nightmares at bay? "Are you trying to get rid of me?"

"Who would I sleep with at night if you're gone?"

I cocked my head. "I'm sure you'd find plenty of girls who'd like the spot."

"Too bad the one who's got it doesn't want it," he said.

He *was* good. I could totally see how girls would eat up his lines. "Hey, I haven't congratulated you on your award yet."

He shrugged.

"You should feel honored. A lot of MVP winners have gone onto the majors," I explained.

"That's the plan...But, I almost didn't even play here this summer," he said.

"Why?"

"I kind of wanted the summer off seeing as though if I get drafted, I won't have one off again until I retire."

"What changed your mind?"

"My mom pushed me to play. She always says a missed opportunity is a missed journey."

"She sounds like a smart woman."

He shrugged. "It's been just me and her my whole life. So, she always wants me to be my best and reach for the unattainable."

Sam and I had spoken about guys with sisters being good guys, but we hadn't discussed those raised by single moms. They tended to be equally good. "I already like her."

"She's sort of a badass like you. She takes no shit from anyone."

I winced. "Not sure if I should be flattered or insulted that you're comparing me to your mom."

"Sorry," he laughed. "I totally meant the badass thing."

"Come on, MVP," I urged as I turned to head back. "I've put in enough time at this event."

Most people had already cleared out when we returned

to the banquet hall. Gina and Cody were the only two people dancing on the dance floor. I stopped at our empty table to grab my clutch, and I caught Gina's eyes and smiled. There was no way I'd make her leave with me, so I pointed to myself then hitched my thumb toward the door, letting her know I was leaving. She nodded.

I turned to see where Crew went, figuring I'd head home with him. He was at his table. He slipped on his suit jacket, picked up his award, and smiled. He should feel proud. That was the biggest honor of the night.

A girl I remember from the bonfire stepped up to him. He smiled as she pressed herself to his chest. She said something to him as she placed her hands against his chest. Her hands drifted up, and it was like watching a train wreck that I couldn't tear my eyes away from. Her hands slipped behind his head. Then, as if in slow motion, she urged his mouth down to hers.

I quickly spun away. The scene from the first day on my balcony materialized in my mind's eye. *That's* who Crew was. He had one-night stands. He used girls who threw themselves at him. I'd almost started to believe he wasn't that guy. But I'd witnessed it firsthand. I hurried toward the exit, hating that I'd forgotten who he truly was.

"Peyton!" Crew called across the room.

I stupidly glanced over my shoulder to find him maneuvering around tables to get to me with the girl following closely behind him. I shook my head. There was no way in hell I was gonna give him a chance to tell me he was leaving with her. "I'm gonna head out," I said, beating him to it. "See ya later."

"Wait!" he pleaded.

I took off for the door and didn't look back. When I found Sam by the exit with some of his teammates, I felt immediate relief. "Take me home," I said, linking my arm through his and pulling him outside with me.

"Normally, this would excite me," Sam said, keeping pace with me as I sought his car in the nearly empty parking lot. "Sadly, I know I'm not getting any action tonight. Why is that again?"

"Because it would ruin the beautiful bromance we've got going," I assured him as I pulled him toward his car.

"Why do I get the feeling that you're trying to get away from someone?" he asked before opening the passenger door to let me in.

"Because I'm totally trying to get away from someone," I said as I slipped into the seat.

He closed my door, rounded the front of the car, and got in.

"Can I guess?"

"Can you drive?"

In record time, Sam dropped me off. I wanted to get changed out of my dress, but I also didn't want to face Crew whenever he returned. Instead of going inside, I took the path to the backyard. I slipped off my heels and beelined it for the pool house—a place I could be alone. I stepped inside and tossed my heels beside the door on the tile floor, locking the door behind me. The over-sized sofa in there would have to do for the night because there was one thing I was sure about. I would not risk Crew trying to slip into my bed after he'd been kissing some other girl. We may not have been hooking up, but I would not lower myself to being second place to some groupie—especially after I'd confided in him.

God, I was so stupid.

I left the light off in the pool house and shimmied out my dress. I tossed it in the closet where I kept some old T-shirts and beach coverups and threw one on. I laid down on the sofa, curling into a ball underneath a throw blanket. The skylights in the pool house were my favorite thing about it. In the daytime, they let in the light, but at night they captured the stars. I exhaled a long breath as I gazed up at the stars.

Maybe I would catch a flight to Alabama.

If I wanted my life to go back to normal, I needed to be away from the Cape. Away from my father. And, away from Crew.

CHAPTER FOURTEEN

Sunlight filtered into the pool house as I woke from a dream I couldn't quite recall. I knew it hadn't been a nightmare because those usually left me feeling empty inside. I swung my legs off the sofa and sat on the edge, pressing my palms into my eyes and pushing away sleep. Considering the way the night ended, I'd slept well.

I got up and opened the door. The briny air, the crash of waves, and squawking seagulls greeted me.

"Good to see you're not dead in some ditch."

I stopped, my eyes shifting to the poolside where Crew sat on a lounge chair. He was still in his suit pants and white button-down shirt, and his tousled hair was a testament to the damp night air. "Why would I be dead in a ditch?"

"Because you didn't come home."

"I've been home since Sam dropped me off—five minutes after I left the banquet."

"I looked everywhere for you," he said.

"Well, I guess you didn't look good enough since I've been here all night."

"Yeah. I realized that somewhere around three."

"So, it sounds like we got that sorted out," I said, moving toward the house.

"She means nothing to me," he said.

I didn't stop. "Doesn't matter to me."

"God dammit, Peyton!" he yelled.

That stopped me. I turned slowly to look at him with narrowed eyes.

"I know what you think of all of us, and I completely understand why. But I just need you to know it meant nothing. And, *nothing* happened."

"And I'll say it again. It doesn't matter to me." With that, I turned and walked inside the house.

"Good morning," my father said from a stool at the island.

Ugh. From one asshole to another. "Not really," I muttered as I moved to the refrigerator.

"I saw you dancing with Crew last night. You two getting along?"

Did he seriously not overhear what just happened beyond the door?

"Nope," I said, grabbing a bottle of water and slamming the refrigerator closed. I walked out of the kitchen and made my way toward the stairs. "He's just like the rest of you," I called.

I walked to the shops, visiting the gift shop where I'd bought my necklace. I reached for the small shells around my neck, brushing my fingers over them for good luck. An hour later I was the newest employee at Hidden Gems and Gifts. My boss couldn't promise me a lot of hours, but she said she could use me for shelf stocking. Today, I was folding Cape

Cod sweatshirts.

"If I didn't see it with my own eyes, I wouldn't believe it," Gina said as soon as she walked inside the shop.

I glanced around, making sure no customers heard her, but they were all busy trying on Cape Cod hats and jewelry at the counter.

"What went down with you and Crew?" she asked.

"What do you mean?" I asked as I refolded a sweatshirt one of the customers had just tried on and discarded in a ball.

"Well, your cryptic text about getting a job tells me that you're majorly trying to avoid him."

I huffed, embarrassed to have to admit that I lowered my guard and it bit me in the ass. "Let's just say, I plan on keeping myself busy for the rest of the summer."

"You couldn't have just gone to the beach? You had to go and get a job?" she asked.

I shrugged. "It's just all getting to be too much."

"Peyton, you know I'm here for you."

"I know." I lowered my voice. "Did you want to buy something?"

She laughed. "I can take a hint."

"I don't wanna give my boss any reason to fire me on my first day," I whispered.

Gina held up her hands. "I get it. Are you coming to the game tonight? It's an away game, so we have to leave early."

"No."

"Come on," she pleaded. "Don't make me go alone."

"You can sit with the Delaney's," I offered.

"Come to the game. We can sit away from the field and wear disguises if you want. I just need to be there for Cody."

"Disguises?"

"Yeah, remember that summer we wore wigs?" she asked.

"We were six."

"Come on. It'll be fun."

I considered her offer. It could be fun to let loose as someone else. "I'll think about it."

She screeched, causing everyone including my boss to look over.

"You need to go," I urged.

"Going," she said loudly, so everyone in the shop could hear. "Pick you up at four."

"Go!"

"I'll bring the wigs." She laughed as she hurried out of the shop.

CHAPTER FIFTEEN

I caught my reflection in the passenger window as I stepped out of Gina's car. I was unrecognizable in my pink wig with sharp bangs.

"Ready?" Gina asked, stepping out of the car in her long blonde wig, a Sharks T-shirt, and cutoffs.

"I never thought I'd see the day when your sundress was replaced by cutoffs and a T-shirt."

We found a spot in the right field bleachers near a team of little league baseball players who were shouting at the players on the field to give them a ball. To survive the game, I'd brought a cocktail in a large tumbler and was having more fun than I expected. It was freeing to be someone else.

"Do you think Cody recognized you yet?" I asked Gina in the bottom of the second.

She shook her head. "He's not even looking out here."

"Well, you told him you'd be here. So, he knows you're here somewhere."

"I might go say hi during the seventh inning stretch," she said.

"Wig and all?" I asked.

"Who knows. He might like me as a blonde."

I laughed and took a sip of my drink. "He'd like you with any color hair. The guy spends every free minute with you."

She blushed, and I knew she needed to hear that—even though it was blatantly obvious to anyone who saw the two of them together. "So, you never told me what happened last night with you and Crew," she said, swiftly changing the subject.

"And here I was thinking that you hadn't brought it up on the drive here, so maybe you'd forgotten."

"I forget nothing," she assured me as something happened on the field and everyone cheered.

I looked to see what it was. Crew dove and stopped a grounder. He got to his knees and fired the ball to first base, getting the runner out with no time to spare.

"I told him about my father," I admitted.

"Oh," she said.

"Yeah. Stupid. I know."

"No, it's just...you keep that one so close to the vest. I'm surprised you felt comfortable opening up to him."

I shrugged. Same.

"But, Peyton," she continued. "It never should've been your secret to keep. Your dad did it. He needs to deal with the aftermath. Not you."

She was right. Why did I hide what he'd done? If he was so worried about his image, he wouldn't have cheated on my mother in the first place. "Yeah, well, so much for opening up to someone. He turned around and kissed some girl in front of me."

"*Seriously?*"

I sipped my drink. "So I had Sam bring me home."

"God, I hate baseball players," she said. "Except Cody of course."

"Of course," I agreed.

"Have you spoken to him since?"

"Yeah. Of course he said it meant nothing. But I told him I didn't care."

"Do you?"

"Why would I?"

"Because there's something going on between you two. I think you need to figure out what it is."

"There's nothing going on."

"Excuse me," one of the little leaguers interrupted, pulling our attention to him standing in front of us. "The shortstop asked me to give the girl with pink hair this ball." He held a baseball out to me. It read *Go Out With Me* in black marker.

I looked out at the field. Crew was staring my way. I looked back at the little kid. "You can tell him he can save it for someone who wants it."

The little boy scrunched his nose. "O-kay."

I looked to Gina who knowingly stared at me with a raised brow.

The little leaguer turned and ran off. But he returned during the next inning still clutching the baseball. "He said you didn't answer his question."

"No," I said.

"He thought you'd say that. That's why he's gonna hit a homer right over here, so you better be ready to catch it since it's for you."

My teeth clenched together as I looked back out at the field. Crew was looking my way again. I hoped the batter hit one right off the side of his face.

"You two are hysterical," Gina said.

I glared at her. "You think this is funny?"

"Isn't it?" she asked, snatching the baseball away from the kid and examining the message on it.

"Do you need my glove?" the little kid asked me.

"What for?" I asked.

"To catch his homer," he explained.

I balked. "You really think he knows where he's hitting that ball?"

"Oh yeah. He's awesome," the kid assured me.

"If you only knew," I mumbled.

The inning ended, and Gina handed me the ball she'd taken from the kid. Did Crew really think sending a kid to ask me out would work? He probably wasn't even serious. He probably just wanted to get a rise out of me.

The Sharks were up to bat at the top of the sixth, and Crew stepped up to the plate. That son of a bitch hit the first pitch—a home run to the right field bleachers. Luckily, the little leaguers had gloves, and one of them caught the ball. As Crew rounded first base, his eyes were on us. I wanted to stand up and remind him about his coach's speech. How he appreciated Crew not prancing around the bases when he hit a home run. Because, at the moment, he was very much gloating as he stared my way and trotted around the bases.

"Can you even believe the nerve of him?" I asked Gina as we drove home after the game.

"It was pretty *ballsy*," she laughed. "He clearly likes you."

"Likes annoying me," I said, drinking my newly-filled cocktail in my tumbler.

"It wouldn't be the worst thing if you two went out."

"Yes, it would."

"Peyton, no one said you had to marry him."

"I'm definitely not manifesting that like you."

"Shut up," she laughed. "Just hear me out. Summer's going to end. He's gonna head back to school and so are you."

"The *same* school," I reminded her.

"It's a big school," she reminded me. "You never have to see him again if you don't want to."

"I don't want to see him *now*."

"You're such a liar."

I grunted.

"He's hot, and I bet he knows what he's doing under the sheets," Gina said.

"Did you seriously just say under the sheets?"

She laughed. "I did."

"It's not like it wouldn't be the first time we've slept in the same bed," I said.

All of a sudden, Gina lurched the car to the right and we swerved off the road. I grasped for something to hold onto as Gina slammed the gear into park, then twisted to look at me. "*What?*"

I shrugged, not really sure what else to say now that my heart was lodged in my throat and my anxiety had shot through the roof.

"Why is this the first I'm hearing of this?" she nearly cried.

"It didn't mean anything."

"Bullshit," she said. "*Peyton.* Why haven't you told me?"

"It was stupid. Neither of us would budge from leaving my room. It started as a challenge..."

"It *started* as a challenge? What is it now?" she asked.

"It's not every night. I slept alone last night."

"Jesus Christ, Peyton. Has anything happened?"

"Define happened," I said.

"Oh my God," she said. "You're in deep."

"Am not."

"Fine. Sleep with him and get it out of your system. Then move on."

I drew back, shocked by her words.

"It's inevitable. And once it happens, you can either go your separate ways or..."

"Or what?"

"Keep doing it."

CHAPTER SIXTEEN

Gina's words played through my head as I entered the pool house after she dropped me off. I plopped down onto the sofa with the ball clutched in my hand and leaned back into the cushion. I couldn't believe she thought Crew and I had something to get out of our systems. He was a *baseball* player. And, I wanted nothing to do with cocky, untrustworthy baseball players...no matter how good looking they may have been. Or, how yummy they might've smelled. Or, how hot they may have looked in their uniforms.

There was a huge splash in the pool.

I sat up, hesitant to look outside for fear of what I might find. But my curiosity got the best of me, and I peeked out the window. Crew emerged from the water, pushing his hair out of his face. I ducked down so he didn't see me.

There was another splash.

Had he seriously brought someone home with him? That son of a bitch.

I pushed myself back up and peeked out to determine if he was alone or had someone with him. As far as I could see, it was just Crew. I ducked back down, feeling oddly relieved, and let him do his thing. It was his home too—at least for the rest of the summer.

Minutes passed.

I waited for the splashing to end, but the guy could do some serious laps.

Eventually, there was silence.

Had he finally decided to go inside the house?

The handle on the pool house door rattled.

Shit.

I knew I locked it, but could he see me through the French doors? I lay still and held my breath.

"I can see your pink hair," he said.

I turned my head to see him standing outside in his swim trunks with his hands cupping his eyes against the glass door. *Dammit.*

"Open the door," he said.

"Sorry, the pool house is occupied."

"Let me in, Peyton," he ordered, and I hated the way my name rolled off of his tongue so smoothly.

"I'm not alone," I lied, not out of immaturity but out of self-preservation.

"Bullshit."

"He plays for the Stingrays."

He dropped his hands and tried the handle again to no avail. "I know you're alone."

"You can have my room. We're good in here."

He lowered his voice. "Open the damn door, Peyton."

"If you think demanding me to do anything is the way to go, you definitely don't know me."

He groaned in frustration. "Will you please open the door. I need a towel."

Shit.

Now I was embarrassed.

He wasn't even looking for me.

I tucked the baseball under the cushion and stood up, grabbing a beach towel from the pile on a nearby shelf. I unlocked the door, cracked it open, and pushed the towel toward him. Crew grabbed the towel with one hand and pushed open the door with the other so that I stumbled back but didn't fall. He closed the door and looked around at the *empty* pool house.

His eyes slid to mine, and he stalked toward me. I backpedaled until I hit the wall behind me. He tossed the towel aside and lifted his wet hands to my cheeks. His blue eyes locked on mine as pool water dripped down his face. "I'm done."

"What's wrong? Upset I didn't fall for the this-ball's-from-the-shortstop routine?"

He shook his head and drops of water from his hair dripped onto my face. "I'm done waiting for you to figure your shit out."

"Great. Then go."

He moved closer, his lips a mere whisper from mine. "I'm going to kiss you."

"Don't."

"Because you don't want me to?" he asked, his breath tickling my lips. "Or because you know as well as I do that we won't be able to stop once we start?"

A ripple rolled through my belly.

"Well?" he prompted, his nose grazing mine. "Which is it?"

My heartbeat thrashed against my chest.

"I would never force myself on someone," he said, his lips almost brushing mine.

My words were a garbled mess in my head. Had he asked me another question? Had I answered his first?

"But know this. I want you, Peyton. You challenge me and turn me the fuck on. And even with this stupid pink wig on, I can't see anything but your pretty eyes. And the way you—"

I crashed my lips to his, my tongue pushing between his lips. He dropped his hands to my hips and urged me closer. I slid my arms over his shoulders, arching into him as his tongue melded with mine in an eager dance. Both of us groaned, our pent-up frustration culminating in this one intoxicating kiss. He lifted me right off my feet, and I wrapped my legs around his hips. He carried me to the sofa and lay me down, covering me with his soaking wet body. His elbows bent at my head as he devoured my lips, his erection pressing through his swim trunks and into my thigh.

He pulled out of the kiss and stared down at me, his chest heaving in tandem with mine. "Did someone drink tonight?"

"Maybe," I said.

"This was not how I envisioned this playing out."

"Did you envision rose petals on the bed and music playing in the background?"

He smiled, and when he smiled like that, summersaults flipped in my belly. "I kinda don't picture you needing that."

"I kinda don't picture you doing it," I sassed.

He pulled the pink wig off my head and tossed it aside. "You'd be surprised at the things I'd do for someone like you."

My brows shot up. "Someone like me?"

He leaned his head down and trailed butterfly kisses down the side of my neck. "Someone sassy…"

I closed my eyes, savoring the soft brush of his lips on my skin.

"And strong," he whispered trailing kisses back up to my ear.

I sighed, sensations swirling low in my belly as he nibbled on my earlobe.

"Someone who's not afraid to speak their mind," he whispered, his tongue circling my lobe.

Even with his weight on me, my chest heaved.

"And, someone hot as hell."

That was it. I reached down and pushed at the waistband of his swim trunks. He took the cue and shoved them down and off his feet.

I reached for the button on my cutoffs. Sensing what I was doing, Crew lifted his hips. I wiggled out of my shorts and panties, then slipped off my bra and T-shirt.

"You wearing nothing but your pretty necklace is going to be a vision I'll never be able to unsee," Crew said lowering himself back down on me.

Once we were skin to skin, the reality of what we were about to do sent a shiver coursing over me.

"You sure about this?" he asked, looking directly into my eyes.

"No."

His eyes widened.

"But I have a feeling it's inevitable."

A smile spread across his face. He leaned in to kiss me but stopped abruptly. "Dammit. My wallet's out there."

"Of course it is."

"Give me thirty seconds." He jumped off me, grabbed the towel and wrapped it around his waist as he bolted out of the pool house. He was back within seconds, grabbing the condom from his wallet and tearing the packet open with his teeth. He dropped the towel and rolled on the condom. I couldn't have torn my eyes away if someone paid me. If I was getting the full Crew treatment, this show had to be included.

His eyes lifted to mine and his lips quirked when he caught me looking. He moved to the sofa and lay himself on top of me. His weight pushed me into the cushions as he adjusted himself so we were aligned. The tip of his dick grazed between my thighs. He used his hand to move it along my folds, swiping it from front to back over and over again. I closed my eyes and my head arched back. He totally knew what he was doing.

"I could do this all night," he whispered.

"Not if I kill you first."

He chuckled, but didn't end his torture.

My hands drifted around his hips, over the smooth skin at the base of his spine, and over his ass. I dug my nails in and he groaned.

"You're playing dirty," he murmured.

"Learned it from you."

He stopped moving his dick over my folds and steadied himself on his elbows on either side of my head. "You ready?"

I nodded.

He shifted his hips and thrust inside of me.

My back arched off the sofa, my chest pressing to his. "*God,*" I sighed.

"Not quite," he grunted as his lips found my collarbone, and he buried them there as his hips began to thrust.

I held onto his ass, the feeling of him driving into me over and over again was so damn sexy.

"You feel amazing," he murmured.

I dug my nails in, needing him deeper. His thrusts became harder, but I liked it. My nails drifted up and over his back, the muscles so prominent beneath his silky skin. The area between my thighs began to constrict, sensations coiling tighter and tighter. His shaft brushed my clit. It was all happening so fast. Was this what it felt like when you had pent-up sexual tension with someone?

My nails traveled back down to his ass and I dug them in, urging him on.

I was close. So damn close.

His lips crashed to mine, our tongues melding. Between him being inside of me and his mouth on mine, sensations uncoiled between my thighs sending shivers out to the tips of my fingers and toes. He swallowed what would have been a cry of pleasure as he continued kissing me and thrusting, milking every last bit of my orgasm from my body. Eventually, he broke the kiss and his thrusts became eager.

"*Grrrrrr,*" he groaned as he stilled inside of me.

He lowered himself down onto me. Our chests heaved as we lay connected for a long time in the silent pool house. I wondered if he was thinking what I was thinking. Had what just happened been two people getting something out of their systems? Or, two people who wanted each other?

"Speechless?" I finally asked.

"Just remember who kissed who first," he said into my shoulder.

Silent laughter escaped us both.

"That's the trouble with players. Everything's a game," I said.

"Makes things more interesting," he said.

"Does it?"

He finally lifted his head, and his eyes were half-lidded and content. "How soon until we can do that again?"

"If this is my one night with the player, I better get as much out of it as I can."

"You know that's not how it is with us," he said.

"How is it then?"

He lowered his lips to mine and kissed me slowly. Every part of my body prickled with the slow glide of his tongue. With the way his hand slipped down my side. With his soft content purrs. With the true intent behind his kiss.

CHAPTER SEVENTEEN

I woke up the next morning wrapped in Crew's arms. "Shit." I scrambled away from him and jumped off the sofa.

"What are you doing?" he asked, his eyes not even open yet.

"It's morning."

"So?"

"So." I grabbed my panties and cutoffs from the floor and shimmied them on. "I don't want my father to find us in here." I grabbed my T-shirt and pulled it over my head.

Crew pressed his palms into his eyes. "He has never once caught us in bed together *inside* the house. Why would he find us out here?"

"I don't know," I said, knowing I was overreacting because I was embarrassed—and nervous that our one night was over, despite his reassurances last night.

"And do you actually care what he thinks?" Crew asked, slipping on his bathing trunks and standing up.

I paused. "No."

He moved closer to me and wrapped his arms around my hips. "Then, what are we doing up?"

I laughed uncomfortably, finding it difficult to maintain eye contact. Last night in the dark after some drinks it seemed like a good idea. But, now, in broad daylight, I wondered if we'd made a colossal mistake.

"You're not regretting last night are you?"

"Why would I regret it?" I asked, hating that he always seemed to be able to read my thoughts.

He shrugged. "Just making sure."

"Do you plan on avoiding me?"

He scrunched his nose. "Why would I do that?"

"Keeping up your reputation."

His brows lifted. "My reputation?"

I nodded. "Your one-night stand reputation."

He lifted me off my feet and I yelped. "I guess not since I'm keeping you locked in here all day with me."

"I have to work," I laughed as he sat down on the sofa with me now straddling his lap.

"Work?"

I nodded, not wanting to explain he was part of the reason I'd gotten the job in the first place.

"We have less than a month left here, and you seriously plan to work?" he asked.

Ripples rolled through my belly. Had everything he said last night not just been lines to get me naked?

"Fine," he sighed. "But, I want all of your free time."

I tried to stifle a smile but the damn thing sprang free.

"Will you at least be at my games?" he asked, watching my eyes closely for the truth.

"Will you be hitting me any more homers?"

A smooth smile swept across his lips. "Maybe."

"How many times have you pulled something like that?"

"Something like what?"

"Calling your home run for a girl's sake."

"Just once," he explained.

I rolled my eyes.

"You don't believe me?" he asked.

I shrugged.

"Big mistake doubting me." He stood, picking me right up with him.

"What are you doing?" I asked as I clutched onto him.

He walked us right out of the pool house and to the path to the beach.

"Crew!" I screeched. "What are you doing?"

"Making you believe me."

"I believe you!" I cried, looking around the vacant beach as he stormed toward the water.

"No, please," I begged. "It's going to be cold."

"Well, then you better get ready." He rushed into the water, his arms tightening around me.

The rush of sixty-degree water sent goosebumps scampering over my skin as he moved us into deeper water until we were up to our chins.

He didn't release me, just held me. "This feels nice."

"What does?"

"Being out here knowing not a soul can see us."

"I knew you planned to keep me a secret."

He laughed. "You know what I meant."

Did I?

He pressed his lips to mine and kissed me slowly, the saltwater mixing with our tongues. He was right. There wasn't a soul around, and the fact that we were all alone out there made it more special. We were in our own little bubble and no one could ruin it.

Breathless, I pulled out of the kiss. "Let's go shower."

His brows shot up. "Together?"

"I hope so."

He kissed me hard. "Oh, you are even more incredible than I thought."

I laughed.

"I'll meet you upstairs in five minutes," he said as he released me. "Wouldn't want Marty getting suspicious."

I rolled my eyes at him before making my way out of the water, grabbing a towel on my way by the pool house, and wrapping it around me on my way into the kitchen.

"Where were you?" my father asked, standing by the sink.

"Excuse me?"

"Did you come home last night?"

"Yes."

"You weren't in the guest room," he challenged.

"I fell asleep in the pool house."

"Common decency would've been to text me if you weren't coming in the house."

"Please don't get me started on common decency," I said.

"I fucked up, Peyton!"

I stilled, surprised by his outburst.

"How many God damned times do I have to apologize for it?"

My surprise quickly morphed into anger. "How many *times*? Until I don't have to replay that day over and over again in my head." *Breathe.* "Until it stops plaguing every one of my nightmares." *Breathe.* "Until I can stand the sight of you without it giving me a pit in my stomach." *Breathe.* "Until I say you've apologized enough!" I spun away from him and raced upstairs with my heartbeat pounding in my temples. I reached the guest room and dropped to the edge of the bed, my hands shaking frantically and my chest growing heavier.

How dare he make this my fault?

Breathe.

A door downstairs slammed.

Breathe.

A car out front started.

Breathe.

Tires screeched over the gravel driveway.

Breathe.

There was soft tapping on my door as it slowly opened and Crew peeked inside. "Are you okay?"

I didn't respond because I knew I was far from it.

He slipped inside and closed the door. "I heard what happened."

I bit the inside of my cheek, trying to stop myself from breaking down in front of him.

He sat beside me on the edge of the bed, the weight of him dipping the mattress and pulling me against him. He wrapped his arm around me. "I'm proud of you for standing up to him."

Tears glazed my eyes so I closed them, hating that every run-in with my father sent my emotions so out of whack. I dropped my head to Crew's shoulder. "Why am I like this?"

"Like what?" he asked.

"Damaged."

"You're not damaged. You're hurt. There's a difference."

"What's the difference?"

"Damaged comes that way. Hurt is done to you."

"You're making that up," I challenged.

"I am, but look at it this way. Something damaged might not be fixable. Something hurt definitely is."

"I still don't believe you," I said.

He pressed his lips to the top of my head. "Then I guess I'm just gonna have to show you."

CHAPTER EIGHTEEN

"Your hair's not pink," the little leaguer from the last game said as he stopped in front of me on the host family hill.

"Then how in the world did you recognize me?" I asked him.

"Crew told me it was you," he said.

"Did he threaten to hit me another home run?"

He smiled.

"He did, didn't he?"

He nodded. "He said this time he's goin' yard."

"And, you believe he'll do it?" I asked.

"Crew's the best player on the Sharks. Of course he'll do it."

"He likes her," Gina interrupted.

"Gross," the kid said before taking off to find his seat.

"So?" Gina prompted.

"So, what?"

"So, why'd you ask *me* to come to the game?"

I shrugged.

"*Peyton*," she probed.

"Fine. I took your advice," I said as my eyes latched onto Crew at shortstop. I wished I wasn't visualizing him naked when he looked so damn hot in his uniform.

"Which advice?" Gina asked. "I tend to give a lot of it."

"The part about getting it out of our systems."

She screeched.

I reached over and cupped her mouth with my hand since people around us had turned to look. "I'm gonna need you to calm down."

She nodded.

I slowly removed my hand.

"I can't freakin' believe it," she whispered. "How was it? Amazing? I'm sure it was amazing. Look at the guy. He's like a freaking underwear model."

I pursed my lips. "It was pretty amazing."

"I knew it."

I laughed.

"Are you gonna do it again?"

I nodded.

She screeched.

I covered her mouth as heads turned again. "*Shhhhh.*"

She nodded like a little kid who'd been scolded.

I reluctantly removed my hand. "Girl, keep your calm."

"I'm sorry. I'm just so dang happy for you. I've been worried about you. But now, you're happy. And I want you to stay that way."

I wrapped my arm around her shoulders and pulled her into me. "How'd I get so lucky to have you in my life?"

"Goes both ways," she said as the inning ended and the Sharks jogged off the field.

"When's their next night off?" I asked.

"Next Tuesday. Why? Wanna go on a double date?" she asked.

"I'm not sure if we're *that* official."

"Well, if you want to. We can."

"There's a lot of time between now and Tuesday."

"What's that mean?"

"It means we could go back to hating each other by then," I explained.

On the field, the Sharks were up to bat. Crew stepped into the batter's box. His hands tightened around the grip of the bat, and I couldn't help but envision those hands last night gripping my skin. The uniform's short sleeves molded to his biceps, and my mind shifted to my own hands clutching his skin. The pitcher delivered his first pitch. Crew swung, and the bat connected with the ball. Fans around us jumped to their feet as the ball sailed over the center fielder's head and continued over the fence behind him.

The fans exploded with cheers as I clapped for the impressive hit from my seat.

Crew circled the bases like he had the first time, his head down and the gloating nonexistent. When he reached home, the on-deck batter bumped his fist. He moved toward the dugout and was congratulated by his other teammates. He glanced to me with a slight smirk on his face before disappearing in the dugout.

That smirk just might be the death of me.

"Excuse me?"

I glanced to my side.

The little leaguer stood there with a baseball in his hand. "He said you should never underestimate him."

I rolled my eyes as the boy handed me the ball.

Gina chuckled beside me. "Sounds like he showed you."

I didn't respond. But, I guess he had. In more ways than one.

After the game, Gina and I waited by her car in the nearly empty parking lot. I tossed the home run ball in my hand.

"Where'd you get the ball?" a deep voice asked.

I looked over at Crew. "Some showoff hit a home run."

"Showoff?"

"Big time."

He laughed. "So, you waited for me."

"Actually, we're waiting for Cody," I explained.

"Well, I'll leave you to it," Crew said. "He'll be out in a few minutes."

Gina nodded as Crew turned and walked away.

My shoulders dropped. Where was he going? So much for him wanting to spend all of his free time with me.

He stopped and turned back toward me. "Would you get over here and stop being stupid."

I exhaled. "Why should I?"

He cocked his head. "Because I told you, I want you by my side at all times."

"*Awwww*," Gina cooed.

With my stomach flipping like some middle schooler who'd been kissed for the first time, I walked over to him. He wrapped his arms around me, pulling me flush against his chest before dropping a kiss to my lips.

"I love you two together!" Gina called.

We smiled against each other's lips.

"Don't forget you still owe me that shower," he said.

"How could I forget?"

———

I steadied myself against the wet tiles with both hands as the shower water rained over me. Crew's arm was hooked around my stomach as he thrust into me from behind. I arched my back, pushing my ass closer to him. Even with a condom on, he glided in and out of me as if we'd done this a thousand times before.

"Jesus, Peyton," he grunted.

I could only gasp, as the sensations began to swirl between my thighs, my legs shaking with the impending orgasm. My fingers slipped on the tiles.

"I've got you," he assured me, his arm tightening around my stomach.

"*Gaaaaahhh,*" I groaned as my orgasm tore through me, the tremors coming in waves.

"I'm right there," he said, pounding into me. "*Grrrrrr,*" he groaned before stilling inside me and dropping his forehead to my shoulder. "Un-fucking-believable."

"Maybe you should've stopped fighting with me sooner," I said.

"You think?"

CHAPTER NINETEEN

I walked into the kitchen the next morning to grab a drink before work since I was already running too late to grab breakfast.

My father sat at the island looking down at his phone. He didn't look up. "I just got off the phone with your mother."

"Did she ask you for a divorce?"

He ignored my question. "We both think it's best if you flew down to stay with her for the rest of the summer."

"Excuse me?"

"You clearly don't want to be around me," he said.

"Then *you* leave. Why should I?"

"Because you're the one who's unhappy here," he said.

I walked over and crossed my arms, leaning my hip against the island beside him. "So let me get this straight. *Now* you care if I'm happy or not?"

"What's that supposed to mean?"

"It means you're the most self-centered man I've ever met."

He slapped me across the face.

The hit came hard and fast and my entire face flew to the side, pain crackling though my cheek like ice. I cupped my cheek, unable to believe he'd laid a hand on me.

"What the fuck?!" Crew rushed into the room and moved to my side. "Are you okay?"

I was too stunned to respond.

His eyes cut to my father's. "I don't care who you are, only a weak man lays a hand on a woman. And, this is your fucking *daughter*."

I turned and hurried out of the room with my cheek pulsing and unshed tears glazing my eyes. I didn't get far when I heard Crew's voice in the kitchen.

"Do you have any idea how much pain you've caused her?!" he yelled.

"Leave it alone, Crew," my father warned.

"She's your kid. Get your shit together, man." His voice lowered, and I had to strain to hear. "If you ever lay your hand on her again, I'll break it."

I hurried out of the house before Crew discovered me listening. I'd made it just around the corner from the gift shop when Crew called my name. I stopped and turned.

He jogged up to me. "Are you okay?"

"Of course," I said, trying to appear tougher than I truly felt in that moment.

With pain in his eyes, he lifted his hand and gently cupped my cheek that was still hot and throbbing.

"Don't look so sad," I said.

"I wanted to slam him right through the fucking wall."

"I can handle it," I assured him.

"You shouldn't have to." He stared into my eyes, and I think he was waiting for me to break down.

"I didn't panic," I explained. "I held it together. Do you know why?"

He shook his head.

I leaned into his hand, needing the connection more than I realized. "Because of you."

"But what if I hadn't been there?" he asked.

"But you were," I said, wanting him to know the huge role he played in helping me. I wrapped my arms around his waist and dropped my head to his chest. His familiar sandalwood scent clung to him as he wrapped me in his arms, and held me right there on the sidewalk as tourists walked around us.

"I don't think it's healthy to have to carry everything you've been dealing with," he said.

"I told you. I held it together. It means I'm learning to manage my attacks."

"I just think...I don't know. Maybe you should talk to someone."

I pulled back and looked at him. "Are you saying *you* don't want to be the one I lay all my problems on?"

"You can tell me anything. But I'm talking about someone qualified to help you and give you more ways to cope," he explained.

"I'll make you a promise. If it gets too much for me to handle, I'll look into it."

"Okay."

And, though I agreed to it, I knew I'd be okay if I had Crew by my side.

———

"How much for this blue Cape Cod sweatshirt?"

I glanced up from my spot at the counter of the gift shop. Crew held up a sweatshirt that complemented his blue eyes. It had only been a couple of hours since he'd left me, but I knew he was there to check on me. "Twenty-five dollars."

He dug into his pocket and tossed the cash down onto the counter.

I reached for it, but he placed his hand on mine. I glanced up. "How are you?" he asked.

"I'm good."

He stared at me, looking for the truth.

"I'm *fine*," I assured him.

"Your father left for Boston."

"Left? Or you kicked him out?"

He smiled. "He said he had to work, but he planned to stay longer. He said it was better for everyone that way."

"He wanted *me* to leave," I explained. "That's what started the argument."

"I wouldn't have let you."

"Oh no?"

He shook his head. "Who am I gonna drive back to Alabama with?"

"That's like a twenty-hour drive."

"So?" he asked.

"So, that's over twenty hours in a car together. I'm not sure I can handle that much of you."

He laughed. "I'm pretty sure you can."

I considered us driving that far together. A road trip definitely taught you a lot about someone. Would we argue the whole time or end up closer at the end?

"I have a surprise for you," he said.

"You don't have to do this."

"Do what?" he asked.

"Do something because of what happened," I said.

"I'm not doing anything because of what happened. I'm

doing it because you're my girlfriend, and I want to make you smile."

The word *girlfriend* made my stomach flip over. Crew didn't *have* girlfriends. "I don't recall ever agreeing to be anyone's girlfriend."

He cocked his head, likely realizing I was never going to concede that easily—even if I wanted to. "Well, what's a guy have to do to get you to agree to it?"

"Well...you said you've never had a serious girlfriend before."

"I haven't."

"What makes you think you're ready for one now?"

He smirked. "Seriously?"

I nodded. "What changed your mind?"

"That's easy. You."

I stifled a smile. Oh, he was good.

"So?" he prompted.

"So...what's the surprise you've got?" I asked, changing the subject.

He shook his head. He had to know I was never going to say yes. But, I also didn't say no. "Not now. Later."

I rolled my eyes. He was such a guy.

"No. Not *that*," he laughed, realizing what I thought he meant. "Although, I wouldn't be opposed if you had your way with me later."

I glanced around, making sure no one else was in the shop.

He laughed. "Relax. We're alone."

"Don't you need to leave for your game?" I asked, checking the time on my phone.

"Trying to get rid of me?" He leaned across the counter. "Because—"

"Don't even say there are other girls who would be happy to take my place," I said.

His brows furrowed. "I was gonna say, 'Because I won't let you.' But now that you mention it—"

I grabbed the front of his shirt. "You saw what I did to that chair."

"I love it when you talk dirty to me."

I shook my head and released his shirt.

He laughed. "All right. I'm going. See you at my game." With that, he left the store. But half an hour later, he texted me asking me to stop by the house on the way to his game to grab his ball cap that he'd left on the balcony.

Once my boss came in and relieved me, I stopped at the house and ran upstairs. I had a little time, so I quickly changed into a Sharks T-shirt and cutoffs in the guest room then headed to my room to grab his ball cap. I moved to the closed French doors and threw them open. I froze. A new Adirondack chair sat there. A wooden sign hung on it: *Peyton's Chair*. Small writing beneath it read: *All others will be "thrown" out*.

I closed my eyes and shook my head. This was my surprise? As corny as it was, I appreciated the gesture. Not to mention the nod to my reaction. I laughed as I sat down in it, taking a quick selfie. I sent it off to Crew with a kissy face emoji. *God*. I was becoming Gina.

Crew: Do you like it?

Me: Love it.

Crew: Want to erase some bad memories in it?

Me: Nope.

He responded with a sad face.

There were just some things I'd never unsee. Him and that girl was one of them.

Me: We're more creative than that.

Crew: Damn straight we are.

I laughed, before hurrying off to the game.

CHAPTER TWENTY

M y green go-cart cut off Gina's. I laughed as I came upon Cody's red go-cart. He tried to cut me off on the right, but I snuck inside on the left, making the corner faster than him. Crew was in the lead, but the guys working the track had turned on the red light signifying our last lap. If I was gonna win, I needed to do it now. The loud sputtering of the car filled the air as I floored it, trying to cut Crew off on the inside curve, but Crew inched over, blocking my attempt. I tried going wide, but he moved that way. *Asshole.* I could see the worker waving us over, and I needed to come to grips with the fact that he'd won, and none of us would hear the end of it tonight.

I climbed out of my car, reaching for Crew's extended hand.

"You almost had me," he said.

"MVP on and off the field," Cody said, patting Crew on the back.

"Seriously?" I asked Cody. "Do you think he needs any more ego-stroking than he already gets?"

Cody looked to me curiously. "Someone jealous?"

"Jealous? More like trying to keep his feet planted firmly on the ground."

Crew wrapped his arm around my shoulders and pulled me into him. "These feet aren't going anywhere."

Though it would seem like the ideal situation that we were both heading back to the same school, we had two different lives in Alabama. And, I hoped our summer fling wouldn't end up being just that. A fling.

We followed Gina and Cody into Monty's a short time later with our fingers linked. I spotted some of his teammates playing pool and flirting with girls. I stopped short, causing Crew to do the same.

"What's wrong?" he asked as Cody and Gina continued over to his teammates.

"This might not be a good idea," I said.

"Why not?"

A few of the girls had spotted us and were whispering to each other.

Crew followed my eyes, then squeezed my hand. "I'm here with *you*."

"But you've been with some of *them*," I said.

"I can't change the past, Peyton. You knew who I was when we started this."

"Doesn't mean I have to like it."

"Well, you need to remember that I sleep with you at night. Not them."

I smiled, the soreness between my thighs reminding me of that.

"Let's go get a drink." Crew ignored his teammates and led me toward the bar. Once he grabbed his beer and my Mai Tai, we headed out to a high-top table near the tiki bar in the back.

He reached over and pinched my necklace, running his fingers gently over the small shells.

"We don't have to be alone out here on my account," I said, knowing he'd taken me out back because of my knee-jerk reaction to seeing other girls he may or may not have been with before me.

"Maybe I want you all to myself. Did you ever think of that?" he asked.

"You sure you're not gonna resent me because I've ruined your game."

He smirked. "I still have game. I just use it on one girl now."

"It's more like you *think* you have game," I said.

He lifted his brows. "Do I need to poll the audience?"

"You're so conceited."

"I think you secretly love it," he said.

I sipped my drink, neither confirming nor denying.

He leaned closer to me. "But let me let you in on a little secret."

I leaned closer.

"The second I met you I knew my game was shot."

"Liar."

He shook his head. "The way you handled the situation on your balcony told me I'd met my match."

I rolled my eyes. "Don't even say, 'You're not like other girls.'"

"Fine, I won't say it, but I'll tell you this. Other girls make it easy. I always know what I'll get from them if I want it."

I groaned. "Why are you telling me this?"

"Because *you*. You made me work for it. You made things exciting. You got my blood pumping, and I couldn't wait to see what you'd do or say next."

"Sounds to me like the chase is over," I countered.

He shook his head. "Oh, no. It's just begun."

CHAPTER TWENTY-ONE

"There you are," Gina said, standing at the edge of the pool as I emerged from underwater.

I waded to the side and pushed my wet hair out of my face. "Where're you going?"

"Cody and I are having a picnic lunch before the game," she explained. "I just wanted to let you know I'll pick you up for the game when I get back."

"Okay. Have fun. Don't do anything I wouldn't do."

"Girl, I wouldn't do *most* things you'd do," she said.

I laughed. "Then, do everything I'd do."

She shook her head. "You're such a bad influence."

"That's why you love me."

"True story," she said before spinning away and heading toward her house.

A huge splash of water splattered me from behind. I twisted to see Crew emerging from the water and wading closer to me.

"Hi," I said.

"Hi," he said stopping in front of me and caging me in

with his arms as he held onto the edge of the pool. "*Again,*" he added.

I smirked. He'd made good on spending all of his free time with me.

"What'd Gina want?"

"She and Cody are going on a picnic."

"A picnic? That guy's *good.*"

"He really likes her, doesn't he?"

He shrugged. "He's going on a damn picnic. I'd say he feels something for her."

"If I wanted to go on a picnic, wouldn't you take me?"

"I'd take you. Then I'd *take* you."

"*Uuuuugh,*" I groaned.

He laughed.

I ducked out from beneath his arms and swam toward the steps in the low end of the pool.

Before I could even get one step out of the pool, he hooked his arm around my stomach and pulled me back into him. "Don't," he said.

"Don't what?"

"Don't be mad. I was joking. If you want a picnic, I'll give you a picnic."

"I don't want a picnic," I grumbled.

"Then what do you want?" he asked, his lips brushing my ear from behind sending tingles scampering over my neck.

This to last. You to never look at another girl. You to never cheat. Us to be happy together. "I don't know."

"I think you do," he said, before peppering my wet neck with soft kisses.

"Did my father leave yet?" I asked as my head dropped back to give him better access.

"Sure did," he murmured against my skin.

"What would you say if he caught us out here like this?" I asked.

"I'd say," he said between kisses, "your daughter's amazing…And you're an asshole for hurting her."

I remained silent. It hurt to hear the words leave his lips, but it was the truth.

"But," he continued, "she's a survivor. And she takes no shit from anyone. She's tough but thoughtful, feisty yet sensitive."

"Thoughtful?" I asked, calling his bluff.

"The way you do things for Gina. Come on, you've got to know you're thoughtful like that."

"Sensitive?"

"Even when you're pissed, there's still a vulnerability behind your words. Things affect you whether you show it or not."

"Sounds like you've been paying attention," I said.

"Since the first minute."

I twisted in his arms, wrapping my arms over his shoulders and my legs around his hips. "The first minute?"

He nodded then kissed me, stealing my breath away as he proved his words. He eventually pulled back. "Wait for me after the game tonight."

I wrinkled my nose. "And look like a groupie?"

He laughed. "You're certainly not a groupie. And, I wanna do something with you."

I pretended to consider it. "If I don't get a better offer."

"I knew that kid I kept sending over was gonna try to get your number," he said, playing along.

"He's like ten."

"Never trust a ball player."

A cold chill rushed up the back of my spine.

I could see in his eyes that the words left him before he

even realized what he'd said. He lowered his forehead to mine. "You can trust me, Peyton. I'm falling for you."

A ripple rolled through my belly as words eluded me.

"And trust me. Feelings like this don't just go away."

I swallowed hard.

"Believe me when I tell you, this thing between us is real."

"Careful, player, these lines are starting to work on me."

He smiled. "They're not lines. And, just know, I'm only saying them to you."

Our lips collided. His tongue swept between my lips, the gentle glide of it melding in time with mine. Crew moved us to the side of the pool until my back touched the wall. I could feel his erection and was sure he was going to take me right then and there.

I pulled back. "Whoa."

Our chests were both heaving.

Crew laughed. "You started it."

"Why don't you end it?" I challenged.

And I knew all too well that Crew loved a challenge.

CHAPTER TWENTY-TWO

Once the game ended and all the other fans had cleared out, the big field lights switched off, leaving Gina and me in complete darkness.

Gina looked around. "You sure he wanted you here and not by the car?"

I held up the baseball a little leaguer had delivered with the words *Don't Move* in black marker.

She switched on her phone's light. "Well, I'm not leaving you alone."

"Thanks, Mom, but I'll be okay," I assured her.

"I know you will," she said, and for some reason I knew she meant in all aspects of my life and not just in that moment.

The field house door swung open and a bunch of the players poured out, rowdy and loud. In the light of Gina's phone, Cody spotted us on the hill and made his way over. Gina stood and launched herself into his arms. "Good game!"

He laughed. "Thanks, babe."

She giggled as he placed her down.

Cody looked to me. "Crew should be out in a minute. He's talking to Coach."

I nodded.

"We'll wait," Gina offered again.

"*Go,*" I urged. "He'll be out soon."

Gina contemplated it.

"Go," I repeated.

"Call me if you need me," she said.

"*Okay.*"

Cody dropped his arm over her shoulder and walked them toward the exit.

I lay back on the grass and stared up at the sky. With the darkness all around and no nearby lights obstructing my view, stars speckled the sky like a beautiful work of art. I tried to make out the different constellations—at least the few I knew—and they popped amongst all the others.

"You make a wish?" Crew asked.

"Maybe." I didn't sit up. "How'd you see me?"

"You stand out no matter where you are."

"You and your lines."

He laughed as he sat down beside me. "What'd you wish for?"

"That I'd meet some hot baseball player this summer and he'd—" My words were cut off by his lips sealing over mine. At first the kiss was slow, but then he climbed on top of me and caged me in with his elbows on either side of my head and the kiss deepened.

He eventually pulled back, giving us both a minute to catch our breaths. Even in the darkness, I could see the flush to his cheeks. "That's what you were gonna say, right? You'd meet some hot baseball player, and he'd kiss you so good it would erase all others from your memory."

"You *would* think that."

"Tell me I'm wrong."

I shrugged, not about to feed his ego even if it was the truth.

"Well, finish your thought then," he said, rolling off of me and laying on his back beside me to stare at the stars.

"I was looking for constellations. Not making childish wishes."

"It's not childish to wish on a star. Don't you make a wish when you blow out the candles on your birthday cake?"

"They never came true. So, I stopped making them."

His head dropped to the side so he could see me. "Seriously?"

I met his gaze. "Seriously."

"Well, that's just sad."

I shrugged.

"Your birthday's in September, right?"

"The twenty-fifth. When's yours?"

"June eighth."

"Sorry I missed it," I said.

"You didn't know me then," he said. "*And*, you were out living your best life."

"You make it sound better than it actually was."

"I thought you had fun until your friend ditched you."

"I missed the beach. And American food. And familiar faces."

"But then you got home and had to deal with an annoying roommate."

I laughed.

His fingers found mine in the space between us. "I'm sorry it didn't turn out how you wanted. But for me, it's been the best summer ever."

"Oh yeah?" I asked.

"I played baseball. Lived in a killer house on the ocean. Met a gorgeous girl. And kicked her ass at baseball."

"That never happened."

He sat up, pulling me up with him. "It's about to." He stood and tugged me to my feet. He wore slides but was still in his uniform, the knees of his pant stained with dirt—a testament to the gritty player he was. He picked up his baseball backpack, careful not to hit me with the two bats standing up on either side of it, and led me to the field.

"I never said I could play," I said.

He hooked his bag to the fence outside the dugout and pulled out a bat and ball. "I bet you can."

"Is this what you wanted to do with me?"

He turned to face me. "Sure is."

"I'll take the picnic."

He laughed as he handed me the bat. "You're hitting first." He grabbed his glove then walked halfway to the pitcher's mound and stopped.

"I can barely see you," I argued.

"Well, I can see you. And this ball's white, so you should have no trouble seeing it."

"Great," I grumbled under my breath as I walked to home plate.

"Do you know how to stand?" he called to me.

"If I say no, will you come stand behind me and help me?" I asked, my eyes slowly getting accustomed to the darkness.

I could see the faint trace of a smile on his face. "If you need me to."

"Such a guy." I got into my batting stance and readied up.

"You ready?" he asked.

"The question is are *you* ready?"

He laughed then tossed an underhand pitch right over the plate. I let it go by.

"You're supposed to swing," he called as the ball bounced to the backstop.

"I didn't like the pitch."

"It was a perfect pitch," he argued.

"Well, I didn't like it."

He laughed as I ran to the backstop and retrieved the ball, tossing it back to him. "You ready?" he asked again.

I stepped up to the plate and got back into my batting stance. "Yup."

He again tossed an underhand pitch right over the plate.

I swung the bat, connecting with the ball and hitting it over his head into the outfield. He twisted around and watched it land between centerfield and right field. I dropped the bat and ran toward first base.

"You're a fucking ringer?"

I laughed as I rounded first base. "You just gonna stand there?" I called as I continued running toward second base. "Because you should probably go get the ball if you don't want me to have an in-the-park-home-run."

He began jogging, but instead of running toward the ball, he ran toward me rounding second. I squealed as he grabbed me around the waist and lifted me right off my feet, tossing me over his shoulder. My laughter filled the air.

"I can't believe you can play."

"Did you bring me out here hoping I couldn't?"

"I thought I could teach you a thing or two."

"Such a show off."

He placed me back down on my feet. "I should've known."

"I played softball until college. Have I never mentioned that?" I asked innocently.

"Um, I think you neglected to mention that."

"Well, I can pretend I don't know how to play."

"Nah. I wanna see what else you can do."

"It's still a fair ball, right?"

"You clearly know it is," he said.

I turned away from him and took off for third base so I could finish my home run trot.

"What the hell!" he called as he finally took off after the ball.

CHAPTER TWENTY-THREE

Gina and I waited in the field parking lot after the Sharks' five to one Saturday afternoon victory. I couldn't help noting a group of girls standing by the exit giggling when the players passed by. I tried to keep my look of disgust to a minimum, but the struggle was real.

Cody walked into the parking lot and Gina ran into his arms.

"Great game!" she said.

He laughed. "I need your enthusiasm tomorrow night. Scouts are gonna be here." He looked to me. "Rumor is they're coming to see Crew, but it couldn't hurt to play my best while they're here."

"Does Crew know?" I asked.

"Yeah. That's what Coach is talking to him about right now. He should be out in a minute. They were just wrapping up," Cody said before looking to Gina. "You ready, babe?"

She nodded then looked to me. "Have fun."

I smiled as they walked off.

"Now there's a welcome sight."

I turned to find Crew parting ways with one of his teammates in the parking lot.

"Congratulations," I said as he walked over to me.

"Thanks," he said before pressing his lips to mine. Once he stepped back, his eyes moved to my mom's Jeep behind me. "What's this?"

"I have a surprise for you," I said.

His brows arched. "Did you write me a poem?"

"What? No."

"Will you?" he asked.

"I wrote those when I was a kid."

"Well, they were good. You should write more."

"Maybe one day. But for now, get in." I got behind the wheel while Crew tossed his baseball bag in the backseat and then hopped in the passenger's seat.

It was a short drive through town and almost sunset when we pulled into the marina parking lot. I parked and killed the engine. Crew looked to me like I was going to explain, but I just stepped out. "Come on," I called as I pulled a hoodie from the backseat and took off for the docks.

"Your family owns a boat?" he asked, catching up and keeping pace with me.

"It's obnoxious, isn't it?" I said as we passed by boats of all sizes.

"Not if we're going on it," he said.

"Oh, we're definitely going on it," I assured him.

"You know how to drive a boat?" he asked as we reached the last boat on the dock.

"We're gonna find out," I said, stopping beside the *Grand Slam,* a twenty-seven-foot Boston Whaler. It wasn't a yacht like some of the massive boats in the marina, but it was in pristine condition given my father didn't usually even take it out.

Crew eyed the sleek boat. "Have you seriously never driven this?"

"There's a first time for everything," I said. "Get on board."

Despite my response, he still climbed aboard. "Just don't kill us."

I laughed. "Fine. I know how to drive it. And, we're not going far."

I stayed on the dock and crouched by the cleat, untying the rope from it. "Catch this," I called to Crew who caught it when I tossed it. I hurried to the bowline and untied it from the cleat and spring line, tossing it to Crew as I climbed onto the boat. I moved behind the wheel and started up the motor. "Once I move away from the dock, pull the buoys onboard."

He nodded and looked over the side of the boat for the buoys. Once I hit the throttle and reversed slowly out of the slip, he pulled the buoys onboard and moved beside me.

The sun had yet to set, so an orange glow lit our way as I steered us away from the marina and out into the bay.

"You look incredibly hot handling this thing," he said.

"If I can handle you, I can handle anything."

"Handle *me*?" he asked, stepping behind me and linking his arms around my waist. "I think it's the other way around." He pressed soft kisses to my neck as I steered us toward a small island Gina and I had been to many times before to watch fireworks or have bonfires with the locals.

"Am I gonna get to drive on the way back?" he asked.

"Depends."

"On what?" he asked as I circled the island to the dock on the backside of it.

"On whether or not you admit this is better than baseball in the dark."

He laughed. "So, baseball wasn't a hit?"

I stifled a smile. "Kicking your ass was fun, but I think you're gonna like this better." As we neared the dock, Crew made sure the buoys were out. I slowed the boat, pulling us parallel to the dock. I switched off the motor. There were no other boats which meant we had the small island to ourselves, at least for the time being.

I jumped onto the dock. "Okay, throw me that rope."

Crew tossed me the rope, and I tied it to the cleat. I moved to the bowline and he tossed me that rope which I tied.

"You're good at this," Crew said.

I laughed. "It's not that hard." I climbed back on board and went down to the galley where the bed and kitchenette were located.

"Is there seriously a bedroom on this thing?" Crew asked, peeking down from the top of the stairs.

"Only the best for Marty Richmond," I said, as I grabbed a blanket from one of the compartments and came back up. "Come on." I climbed off the boat and onto the dock. "There's a new moon," I said, unable to conceal my excitement.

"What's that mean?" Crew asked as he followed me to the beach.

"It means it'll be darker," I explained, bumping him with my shoulder.

"Does the boat have lights?"

I looked at him, unsure if he was joking or serious. "You're not scared of the dark are you?"

"What do you think?"

"I think you're a big baby hidden in the body of an athlete."

He turned with a devious look in his eyes and swept me up in his arms and over his shoulder like he had on the baseball field. "Could a big baby do this?"

I squealed. "Maybe."

"Maybe?" he asked incredulously. "Could he do this?"

I screeched as he lifted me *Dirty Dancing*-style over his head. "Put me down!"

He laughed. "I could do this all night."

"You're such a liar. Put me down!" I kicked my legs, but it didn't stop him. Instead, he began trudging unsteadily through the sand with me over his head. "*Crew*! Put me down!"

"Why? I'm havin' the time of my life," he taunted, even though his steps in the sand didn't feel stable.

"Jesus, Crew. You're not a baby," I cried in one nervous breath. "Now, put me down!"

"I think I missed what you said." He stopped with me balanced above his head. "Could you repeat that?"

"I said you're *not* a baby. You're the strongest guy I know."

"Will you write me a poem?"

"*Yes!* Now, *please* put me down."

He swiftly dropped me into his arms, cradling me like a baby.

I gasped with the sudden movement, but I was relieved to be down. Once he lowered me to my feet, I glared at him. "Not funny."

"Oh, I think it was really funny."

I led us along the beach, and since it was nearing eight-thirty, darkness almost cloaked the island. We reached a perfect spot on the beach, so I spread out the blanket and sat down, knowing the tide wouldn't come up that high.

Crew sat down beside me, looking out at the horizon. "We missed the sunset."

"Well, lucky for you, that's not why we're here," I said, slipping off my flip-flops.

He hooked his arm around my waist and pulled me into his side. "Did you have something else in mind?"

"Yeah. I've got something to show you that's gonna blow you away."

He looked around the beach. "Well, where is it?"

"It's not something that you can rush," I explained.

"Well, then, while we've got this whole deserted island to ourselves..." He lay us back so we both stared up at the stars filling the sky. This night sky was even more exceptional given the sliver of moon gave off minimal light. "Maybe we'll see a shooting star."

"So I can make a wish that won't come true?"

"You're breaking my heart," he said.

"Why?"

"Because if you never wish for anything, what's the point?"

"What'll *you* wish for?" I asked, turning it on him.

His head fell to the side. I met his gaze. "Getting drafted top ten in next year's draft."

"Cody said there are scouts coming to see you play tomorrow night."

He shrugged.

"That's a big deal," I assured him.

"Only if I deliver."

"I'm probably gonna regret saying this, but..."

"But what?" he pried.

"You're one of the best players I've seen come out of the Cape League since I've been going to games."

"You don't have to say that," he said.

"I'm serious. Your coach was right about the type of player you are. You have this quiet intensity and this innate athletic ability that not everyone's born with."

His eyes flashed away as if I was embarrassing him.

"You better not change when you're a famous baseball player. Or, forget me."

He closed the distance between us and captured my lips. I let him kiss me. Let him show me that he heard me and believed me—and wouldn't forget me. Without breaking the kiss, I climbed on top of him, straddling his hips. I deepened the kiss, taking charge and grinding on him. He grabbed for the hem of my shirt, but I stopped him. I pulled back, and we were both breathless. "Not right now," I chided.

"Seriously? You can't just take advantage of me like that and then pump the breaks."

"Why not?"

"Because you're being a tease."

I laughed but didn't give in, rolling off of him instead. I looked out at the water and shrieked, "Oh my God!" I jumped to my feet.

"What?" Crew asked, jumping up beside me.

I pointed out at the water. "Look." I rushed to the water's edge. A swirling blue iridescent glow ran the length of the shoreline.

"What is it?" Crew asked, stepping up beside me and staring at the beautiful glow.

"It's bioluminescence. Isn't it beautiful?"

"It's amazing," he said, awed by the otherworldly display. "It's like the Northern Lights in the water."

"It's plankton. They produce light through a chemical reaction." I walked knee deep into the water. "Come on."

Crew shucked his sneakers and socks and rushed into the water, creating more swirling blue light.

"When you stir up the ground," I explained, "it reveals more of them."

"This is the coolest thing I've ever seen."

I smiled, loving that I could share this experience with him. "Best date ever?" I asked.

"Close second to baseball in the dark."

I reached down and splashed a handful of water at him. "*Liar.*"

He retaliated, splashing me with even more water.

I tried to get away but he lunged forward, hooking his arm around my stomach. I laughed as he pulled my back to his chest. I spun to face him, and before I knew it, he'd scooped me up in his arms. I wrapped my legs around his hips and draped my arms over his shoulders. He stared into my eyes as the iridescent glow swirled all around us.

"You're so pretty when you laugh like that."

"I laugh all the time."

He shook his head. "Not like this."

"Maybe I'm happy."

He stifled a smile. "I'm glad."

"Aren't you?" I asked.

"Very."

My eyes narrowed. "What aren't you saying?"

"Don't you know?" he said, a shyness sweeping over him.

"Know what?"

A shy smile swept across his face. "That I'm done."

I tipped my head. "Done with what?"

"Ever looking at another girl again."

"*Right*," I said, knowing he always had the best lines.

"I'm serious. No matter where we are, all I can see is you."

My heart flipped over in my chest as I assessed the seriousness in his eyes. There was no trace of it being a line. No trace of him being insincere. My lips crashed to his. And he made sure to show me, right there in the bioluminescence, that all he could see was me.

CHAPTER TWENTY-FOUR

I awoke to the sun shining through the pool house skylights. Crew shifted beside me on the sofa, tightening his arms around me and pulling me closer into his chest. "Morning," he murmured.

"Morning."

"I can't think of a better way to wake up on the biggest day of my baseball career."

I smiled. He was totally going to impress the scouts tonight. There was no way he wouldn't.

"Last night was amazing," he said, burying his nose in my hair. "Thanks for taking me to see it."

"Thanks for going with me."

"I'd go just about anywhere with you," he said.

"Oh yeah? Where wouldn't you go?"

"The woman doctor."

"You mean the gynecologist?"

"Yeah. And I wouldn't go to a nail salon."

I laughed. "Is that it?"

He pursed his lips, considering my question. "I think

that covers it. I really don't wanna get up, but I've gotta lock in if I'm gonna be my best tonight."

"Don't let me stand in your way," I said, even though I didn't want him to leave yet.

"Two more minutes," he said, holding me tighter.

"Do you want me to make you a sign tonight?"

"A sign would be nice. Or, you could wear my away jersey. You'd look good in my number."

"I could do that," I agreed.

"Will you do that when we get back to school, too?" he asked.

"If you plan on seeing me when we get back," I said.

"I guess we'll have to just wait and see," he mused. Feigning anger, I attempted to pull out of his arms, but he held on. "Of course I'm gonna see you."

"So, what should I expect? Lines of girls waiting for you outside of your classes?"

"And, large groups gathered around me at meals. I mean, I can't really help it if they're all just trying to catch a glimpse of greatness."

I rolled my eyes. "You're so dumb."

"Oh yeah?" He pressed kisses all over my face.

I giggled until he stopped.

"We're gonna have a hell of a senior year together. Okay?"

I nodded, hoping he didn't feel like I constantly needed reminders that he wasn't like my father.

He finally released me and rolled off the sofa. He pulled on his clothes from last night. "I'm gonna grab a bagel. You want one?" he asked, tossing me my clothes.

"Sure," I sat up and pulled them on.

He followed me out of the pool house and to the back door. I stepped into the kitchen, stopping short which caused Crew to stop behind me. A woman I'd never met before stood beside my father who sat on a stool. A cold chill rushed up the back of my neck as I looked between them. The woman was younger than my mom and had beautiful blue eyes and blonde hair.

My hands began to tremble and my heart began to race. "What the hell is this?" I asked, my chest tightening with each breath.

"Peyton?" my father said, jumping up from his stool.

"You *asshole*! How could you bring some whore into our house?!" I spun away, pushing past Crew in the doorway and rushing outside, desperate to catch my breath. Was he fucking serious?

Breathe.

I made it to the beach and dropped to the sand.

Breathe.

Had he been cheating all along?

Breathe.

Had he made me out to be the bad guy for not forgiving him when he'd been unfaithful all along?

"Peyton?" Crew called as he ran out from the path onto the beach. "Are you all right?" He knelt in front of me and grabbed my hands. "Breathe, baby."

I tried. I really did.

"It's not what you think," he said. "That was my mom."

I blinked hard. "What?"

"Back at the house. That was my mom."

Embarrassment washed over me. "What?" I repeated, my breath returning to me.

"Come on." He ticked his head toward the house. "I want you to meet her."

Even though the air returned to my lungs, my eyes widened. "No."

He laughed. "No?"

"I just called your mother a whore. There is no way I'm going back in that house."

"I'll explain why you said that. She's cool. She'll get that it was a big misunderstanding."

I shook my head. "I can't."

"So, you don't want to meet my mom?" he asked amused.

"I do. But I need time."

"How much time?" he asked.

"Until I don't want to die."

He laughed. "Fine. But I really gotta get back to her. I took off before I found out why she's here."

"Please apologize for me."

"Of course." He leaned forward and kissed me. "This is gonna go down as a classic story someday." He climbed to his feet and took off for the house. "If you change your mind," he called.

"I won't," I called.

His laughter followed him until he disappeared on the path.

I fell onto my back and lay there for a long time feeling mortified that my outburst was the first impression his mom would have of me. There was no changing that. It happened.

I texted Gina and informed her of what I'd done. She let me hide out at her house until it was time to get ready for the game. Only then did I head back to my house. I tiptoed inside and silence surrounded me. I breathed a sigh of relief.

I climbed the stairs to the second floor and stopped in my room. I expected Crew to have left his away jersey out for me, but since he hadn't, I opened his top drawer: boxers and socks. I opened his middle: shorts and T-shirts. I opened his bottom: baseball pants and his jerseys. I knew they wore white on the road for away games, so I nabbed that jersey. I wondered why his home jersey was in there. Did he have two?

I dressed in the jersey, cutoffs, and sneakers. If I was gonna re-meet his mom, I wanted to look my best. I curled my hair and swiped on some makeup. My necklace kept catching on the jersey, so I removed it and left it on the dresser, then met Gina out front.

"Look at you," she said when I stepped up to her car.

"Crew wanted me in his jersey."

"That's super cute," she said. "You ready to meet the mother again?"

"Ready as I'll ever be," I said, knowing I'd have to face her sooner or later.

Once we arrived at the field, we made our way to the first base line. "Do you see her?" I asked, my eyes on my feet for fear of dying of embarrassment.

"You said blonde and blue eyes?" Gina whispered.

"Yes."

"I don't see any woman fitting that description," she said.

I lifted my head and looked around. Gina was right. His mom wasn't around.

We opened our chairs and settled in amongst the host families.

"Peyton," Sam called, leaning against the fence down on the field. "Nice shirt."

I smiled.

"Sucks about Crew," he said.

"What about Crew?"

"That he's sick," Sam said as if I should've known.

I stood and moved toward him. "Sick?"

"That's what Coach told us."

My eyes moved to the players behind Sam playing catch. "He's not here?"

"You didn't know?" he asked.

"I haven't seen him since this morning."

"Well, I hope he's okay. We've only got a few games left, and there's no telling if the scouts will be back."

Sam jogged into the outfield while I stood confused. Crew was fine this morning. What happened between then and now that would keep him from playing in front of the scouts who were there for him?

I pulled out my phone and texted him as I walked back to Gina. **Where r u?**

"What'd Sam say?" she asked.

"Crew's not here," I explained.

"Where is he?"

"I have no idea. Sam said he's sick, but he wasn't at home. I went in his room."

"Do you think he went to his mom's hotel?" Gina asked.

"I just texted him. He hasn't responded."

"Call him," she urged.

I did. But my call went straight to voicemail. "Crew, it's me. Call me when you get this."

"This is weird," Gina said.

I stood up. "Can I have your keys?"

"Where are you gonna go?" she asked as she handed me her keys.

"I need to check the pool house."

She nodded. "Call me when you find him."

I jogged away from the field, passing groups of people walking in the direction of the field. I stepped into the parking lot and hurried to Gina's car, pulling open the door and getting in.

I noticed a piece of paper on the passenger seat. I snatched it up.

I'm sorry.

I flipped the paper over, but nothing was written on the other side. I'd sat in that seat on the way to the field and that paper wasn't there. Had Crew shown up? Had he left this without playing in one of the most important games of his life? But why? And, what was he sorry about?

I was completely lost.

I tried his phone again. When his voicemail picked up, I began to speak. "Crew, it's me again. I'm worried. I'm at your game, and you're obviously not here. Sam said you're sick, but you were fine this morning. Does this have to do with what happened with your mom? Did she want you away from me after the way I treated her? Was it my father? Did he give you trouble?" I looked at the note in my hand. "And what's with this note? I'm really hoping it's not from you because that would mean you came by the field but didn't stay. What would make you not show up for a game? A game that had scouts wanting to see you play. You're the MVP. Your teammates need you…I need you." My eyes glazed with tears, so I ended the call and tossed my phone onto the passenger seat.

I started the engine and sped out of the parking lot. I was home in minutes. I hurried around to the patio and rushed to the pool house. I threw open the door only to find it empty. *Dammit.* I jogged into the house and climbed the stairs to the second floor. I opened my bedroom door. Everything looked like it should.

I looked to his dresser. The one I'd gotten his jersey

from an hour before. I grasped the handle on the top drawer. I pulled it open. It was empty. My heartbeat began to hasten. I tried the middle. It was empty. A sinking feeling filled my stomach. I tried the bottom. It was empty. Sweat beaded on my forehead.

Breathe.

I moved into the bathroom and pulled open the shower. His shampoo, body wash, and razor were gone.

Breathe.

I dropped to the floor and buried my face in my knees.

He said I could trust him.

He said he wouldn't hurt me.

So, where the hell was he? And what was he sorry about?

CHAPTER TWENTY-FIVE

A voice in the kitchen carried its way upstairs waking me from my spot on the bathroom floor. I struggled to open my eyes given all the tears I'd shed, but once I did, I realized sunshine filled the room. I grabbed my phone from the floor beside me only to find no calls or texts. The voice downstairs continued. I pushed myself to my feet, a little achy from my night on the floor, and hurried downstairs. "Crew?" I called as I stepped into the kitchen.

My father sat at the island on the phone.

I exhaled, disappointed to find him and not Crew. "Where's Crew?"

"I've gotta go," he said into the phone before placing it down on the island.

"Have you talked to him?" I asked.

He shook his head. "He took off after his mother showed up. We didn't know where he was going."

"What'd she say to him?"

He shrugged.

"Did he seem unhappy to see her? Because when I saw

him, he wanted to go talk to her. What changed? Did they have a fight?"

"Look, you're asking the wrong person."

"The wrong person?" I asked incredulously. "You were the only one here when he saw his mom. Who else should I ask?"

"Did you call him?" he asked.

"He's not answering his phone," I explained. "Could his mother have taken him home?"

My father shrugged. "She left alone after he did."

"This is insane. He wouldn't just disappear like this. Especially when he had scouts coming to see him."

"Why are you so concerned over a guy you wanted out of our house?" he asked.

"The better question is why aren't *you*?"

———

I sat behind the counter of the gift shop staring down at my phone. But, no matter how long I stared at it, neither a text nor call came through.

"How much for this T-shirt?" a customer asked.

I didn't bother looking up. "All T-shirts are fifteen dollars."

"I'll take these two," he said.

I cashed him out, bagged the shirts, and continued looking at my phone.

"Anything yet?" Gina asked, stepping into the store a short time later.

"Nothing. Has Cody heard anything?" I asked, a trace of hope in my tone.

She shook her head as she stepped up to the counter.

"None of the guys have. But I was thinking. If they win tonight, they're in the championships game this weekend."

"So?"

"So, maybe Crew will show up for that," she offered.

"He missed playing in front of scouts. Why would he come back for a game?" I asked.

"None of this makes any sense," she said.

"Maybe he played me."

"*Peyton.*"

"Maybe his first impression of me never faded. Maybe us being together was just a nasty game. Maybe it was payback for me flipping out that first day."

"If it really had been to get back at you, why disappear before his opportunity to play in front of the scouts? If this was about you, why would he miss *his* big shot?"

"That's what's so crazy," I said. "Will you do me a favor?"

"Anything."

"If he by some slim chance shows up at the game tonight, will you call me?"

"Of course," she said.

———

I lay in my bed feeling more alone than I had in a long time. Even the crashing of ocean waves outside my window did little to calm my mind. I picked up my phone and called my mom. She answered on the second ring. "Hi, sweetie."

"Are you busy?"

"I'm never too busy for you."

I sighed.

"Uh oh. What's going on?" she asked.

Where did I even start? My boyfriend disappeared. I've

been having panic attacks. Dad slapped me. "I started dating someone."

"That's great!" she said, excited for the details. "Who is he?"

"Well...actually...the baseball player we're hosting. Crew."

Her tone instantly changed. "Does your father know?"

"Why is it any of his business?" I asked.

"Because the two of you are dating and living under the same roof. Can't you see how that could be a bit of an issue?" she asked.

"Well, there's nothing for either of you to worry about," I explained. "He left."

"What do you mean he left? The season's not over yet."

"His mom showed up, and I accused her of being a whore."

"*What*?!"

"I guess you could say I jumped to conclusions."

"I'll say. Was Crew upset over that?" she asked, trying to understand what one thing had to do with the other.

"That's' the thing. He wasn't. He said he'd explain everything to her. And then he disappeared."

"What do you mean he disappeared?"

"I went to his game, and he wasn't there. When I came back home, all of his stuff was gone. I tried calling him, but he hasn't returned any of my calls or texts. His teammates don't even know where he went."

"Does your father know?" she asked.

"If he does, he's not saying."

"Oh, honey. I'm sorry. There's got to be a good explanation. No guy in their right mind would leave you without a good reason."

I closed my eyes, wishing she was right.

"I'm flying up," she said.

"No. Stay with Grandma."

"I can be there by morning," she assured me.

"I know. But there's nothing you can do. I don't think there's anything anyone can do." He'd left. He'd cut off contact. He'd broken my already broken heart.

CHAPTER TWENTY-SIX

"You did not hear this from me," Gina said as she swooped into the gift shop two days later.

I stood from where I was crouched fixing shirts on a bottom shelf. "Hear what?"

"He's staying with DePetrillo."

"What?"

"Crew. He's crashing there."

My mind reeled, and I couldn't believe my ears. "He's still on the Cape? Is he all right?"

"From what Cody heard, he's not doing a lot of talking. Something's up, but he hasn't told anyone what it is."

"I've gotta go see him." I bolted toward the door.

Gina grasped my arm. "I swore to Cody I wouldn't tell you."

"Why aren't you supposed to tell me?" I asked.

"Because Crew doesn't want to see you."

It was as if the floor had dropped out from beneath my feet. "What? Why?"

She shook her head. "I don't know. That's all DePetrillo

could get out of him. But I figured if you came to the game tonight, maybe you could get some answers."

"But why is he avoiding *me*?"

She shrugged.

"I'm going to the game tonight."

"I hoped you'd say that," Gina said.

———

Gina picked me up at five. The pit in my stomach couldn't have been any bigger. I hadn't eaten all day, and despite it being in the nineties, my hands trembled no matter what I did to stop them.

"Are you okay?" she asked, her eyes moving between me in the passenger seat and the road.

"No."

"You've got this," she assured me.

"Right."

"You'll watch the game, and when it's over, you'll get answers."

"I don't know how I'm gonna be able to sit through the whole game knowing he doesn't want to see me," I admitted.

"You'll do it because you know when it's over, this whole thing will make sense."

"And what if it doesn't?" I asked.

"Then, we figure it out together," she said as she pulled into the parking lot.

My heartbeat began to wallop in my chest as Gina parked her car and we got out.

"Ready?" she asked.

"Nope."

We took our usual spot amongst the host families. Many of the Sharks were out on the field stretching or playing catch, but I couldn't see Crew. I didn't want it to look like I was searching for him, so I sat in my chair and pretended to look at my phone while I kept the field in my peripheral vision.

"Can you see him?" I asked Gina.

"No," she said, blatantly staring out at the field.

"Don't be so obvious," I urged.

"Well, if I can't see him, that means he can't see me."

"Maybe he's not here," I said, glancing up at the field.

She was right. He wasn't out there with the rest of the team.

After the national anthem, the Sharks ran out to their positions. My heartbeat tripped over itself when Crew ran out to short stop. His ball cap was pulled down low like it usually was, and if he was looking at the fans, no one would've been able to tell.

While the pitcher threw warmup pitches, the Sharks first baseman warmed up the infielders. When he threw a grounder to Crew, Crew threw it back to him and then dragged his cleats back and forth over the dirt beneath him, something I'd never seen him do before.

The Whalers' first batter stepped into the batter's box. But my eyes were on Crew. He looked fine. He didn't look like someone who needed to miss one of the most important games of his life. The Sharks pitcher wound up and threw his first pitch. The Whalers' batter swung and hit a line drive to short. Crew stuck out his glove to catch it, but it hit off the palm of his glove and bounced into centerfield. The centerfielder picked it up and tossed it in to second.

Crew punched his fist into his glove.

"Shake it off, Burke," a coach called from the dugout.

Crew didn't look up at him.

The next batter hit a home run over the fence. The fans around me groaned.

Crew dropped to his haunches as the batters made their way around the bases. Instead of one run scoring, two scored because of his error.

The Sharks escaped the inning only giving up those two runs. When they ran off the field toward the dugout, I kept my eyes on Crew. He never lifted his eyes.

Cody led off in the bottom of the first inning with a double. DePetrillo followed him, hitting a single to right field, moving Cody over. Crew was announced next. A lump crept up the back of my throat and lodged itself there as he stepped up to the plate. The crowd grew quiet as the Whalers' pitcher wound up and delivered a nasty slider. Crew swung and missed.

"What's up with him tonight?" a guy seated somewhere behind me asked.

Crew stepped back into the batter's box and got into his stance. The pitcher wound up and delivered a fast ball right over the plate. Crew must've anticipated a curve ball because he swung the bat and missed again.

"Let's go, Burke!" his teammates yelled from the dugout.

Frustrated, Crew shook his head as he stepped back into the batter's box and readied in his stance. The Whalers' pitcher wound up and delivered another curveball. Crew swung with all his might and missed again, striking out. The fans around me groaned as Crew slammed his bat down on the dirt before walking back to the dugout.

I could sense Gina looking at me, but my eyes were on Crew. He didn't look up to where I sat. His eyes remained down as some of his teammates patted the top of his helmet on his way back into the dugout.

In the top of the third inning, there was a runner on first with one out. The Whalers' batter hit a ball right to the Sharks second baseman. He scooped it up and threw it to Crew covering second to make a double play. Crew missed the ball, killing any chance of the double play which would have taken them out of the inning. A few fans around me grumbled while others discussed Crew's bad game.

Crew struck out for his second at bat and when the Sharks ran out for the fourth inning, Crew had been replaced by Pryor at short.

"They benched him," I said.

"Good thing the scouts weren't here tonight," Gina said.

The Whalers won the game 5 to 0. As the Sharks exited the field to the field house, the crowd cleared out.

"What are you gonna do?" Gina asked.

"I'm staying right here."

Gina and I waited for a good half an hour. I couldn't sit still. I was about to jump out of my skin: pissed, nervous, terrified.

The door to the field house finally opened. Almost all of Crew's teammates filed out with their heads down.

Cody came out alone, his eyes cast down and his stride slower than normal.

"You'll get 'em next time," Gina said when he approached us.

Cody smirked. "We don't play them again."

"Well, then, you'll get the next team."

He laughed.

"Where's Crew?" I asked Cody.

"It's not a good time to talk to him, Peyton."

I ignored his warning. "How long until he's out?'"

He huffed, clearly frustrated with me. "He's talking to Coach."

"I can wait."

"I'm waiting with you," Gina said.

"I love you, but I've gotta do this alone," I said. "Will you leave me your keys and have Cody take you home?"

She looked to him and he shrugged. She looked to me. "You sure about this?"

"It has to happen."

She threw her arms around me. "No matter what happens, I'm here for you."

"I'm not dying. I got ghosted."

She stepped back with an unamused look and handed me her keys. "Call me as soon as you talk to him."

I nodded. "Thanks for this."

As Gina and Cody walked toward the parking lot, I sat down on the ground. The lights switched off, cloaking the area in darkness. The door to the field house opened and a few coaches walked out. The beam of light behind them was cut off when the door closed, again leaving me in darkness. Last time when I waited in the dark, I was excited for what Crew had planned for us after the game. Tonight, I was filled with dread.

Minutes passed and no one else exited the field house.

Crew had to be in there.

Was he waiting to be sure we didn't cross paths?

More minutes passed. I reached for my necklace to fiddle with it, but it wasn't around my neck. *Dammit.* I'd taken it off when it kept snagging on Crew's jersey. I'd forgotten that.

I checked my phone. The game had ended an hour ago.

I was done waiting.

I stood up, brushing grass from the back of my shorts. I pulled in a deep breath and took off for the field house, yanking open the door and walking inside. I passed a small office and then stepped into a small locker room. Crew sat on the bench in front of the lockers, his elbows were on his thighs, his fingers were laced together, and his head was bowed.

"I'm glad to see you're not dead in some ditch," I said from the doorway.

He glanced up, and even though his Sharks ball cap was pulled down low, I searched for answers behind his distant gaze. "You sure about that?"

I shrugged. "I guess it depends on why you disappeared."

"I'm sorry."

I stepped into the room. "This is the second time I'm hearing that from you. But newsflash. You packed up and left."

"It's not that simple."

I crossed to the bench across from him and sat down. "I'd say it is. You could've stayed. But you left without any reason."

"I had a reason," he said, his eyes avoiding mine.

"What is it?"

He didn't respond.

"Did you meet someone else?"

His eyes cut to mine. "What?"

"Did you cheat on me?" I asked.

"Why would I do that? I love—" He cursed under his breath.

"You love me?" I pressed.

I watched indecision cross his face.

"What the hell, Crew? Why'd you fucking leave?!"

He scrubbed his hands up and down his face. "No matter how I say it, you're gonna be hurt."

"I'm already hurt."

He stared at me for a long time with exhaustion in his eyes. "I know what your father did to your family destroyed you." His eyes cut away. "It was the worst kind of betrayal."

I shook my head, not understanding what my father had to do with any of this. That's when it hit me, and I gasped. "Did you get someone pregnant?"

His eyes shot to mine. "What? *No.*"

I huffed, frustrated with his inability to come straight out with the truth when it was all that I wanted from him. "I came here for answers. Not to try to guess what's going on with you."

"I don't want you to feel the way I do."

Nothing he was saying was making any sense. I stood and crossed to his bench, sitting down beside him. My arm brushed his, and he shifted away from me. I ignored the literal brush-off and persisted. "How do you feel?"

His eyes cut to mine. "Confused...Sad...Sick."

My head hitched back. "Sick?"

He nodded slowly as if he wished I could read his mind.

"Crew." I placed my hand on his thigh and he jumped up as if electrocuted by my touch. My eyes widened. "What's wrong?"

He melded the brim of his hat into an arc, visibly pained by whatever he had to say. "You were convinced your father cheated with other women."

I nodded.

"Well...he did."

I tipped my head to the side, trying to follow.

"He cheated with my mom," he explained.

I froze as visions of the woman in the kitchen flashed in my mind. "Okay..." I said, trying to be rational though my thoughts and emotions battled for control. "So, I was right about her being there for that?"

He shook his head. "What happened between them happened in the past."

I exhaled, trying to be sensible. "I knew there had to be others...it's why I had the dreams. None of this is really a big surprise."

"But it was *my* mother."

"Your mother. Not you," I assured him.

"*Peyton*," he pled.

"It's okay. You didn't do this. *He* did."

"You're not listening to me."

"I *am*! And I'm okay. The reason you left makes sense now, but you didn't have to leave. We could've dealt with it together. We still can."

He closed his eyes.

I stood up, feeling the need to console him. I cupped his cheeks with my hands. "We can make this work," I whispered. "Look. I'm not even having a panic attack."

"He got her pregnant," he said, his eyes still closed.

I bent at the waist and braced my hands on my thighs, my head beginning to swim. "There's another kid out there?" I murmured, trying my hardest to keep my breathing steady.

Crew didn't respond.

My eyes lifted to his. "You have a sibling?" I asked.

He shook his head.

CHAPTER TWENTY-SEVEN

I stood up straight, keeping my panic attack at bay. "But you just said—"

"I need you to sit down and listen to me and not say anything until I'm done. Can you do that?" Crew asked.

I nodded, lowering myself down onto the bench.

"When I left you on the beach, I went back to see my mom. She and your dad were arguing, and I could tell they knew each other."

I listened, realizing now that my father purposely didn't mention any of this.

"He called her some pretty ugly names so I jumped in and threatened him. That's when my mom spoke up."

"What'd she say?" I asked, unable to hold my tongue any longer.

"She told him..." he began, swallowing hard. "...that he's my father."

Bile shot up the back of my throat. I covered my mouth and bolted into the nearby bathroom, making it just in time to vomit. I dropped to my knees and hugged the toilet bowl.

My head spun and tears flowed from my eyes as I continued to heave.

Did Crew *know?*

Had this been a twisted way to get back at a man who deserted him?

Had I been the pawn in a game I didn't know I was even a part of?

Once every last bit of vomit was wrenched from my body, I sat with my knees tucked up on the floor. With shaky hands, I dabbed my tears with toilet paper and blew my runny nose.

There was a soft knock and then the door opened. Crew slipped inside.

"Did you know who he was?" I asked. "Was this all a twisted way to get back at him?"

"God no," he assured me as he sat down on the floor beside me. "I'm just as shocked as you,"

"Do you swear to me?" I asked.

"I'd never do something like that. This rocked my world too."

I finally understood why he left. Why he hadn't explained. Why he hadn't played in front of the scouts. I dropped my head to his shoulder because, despite what I'd learned, I still needed him—in whatever capacity I could have him. "I'm sorry."

"Why are *you* sorry?" he asked.

"Because I should've trusted you. I knew you never would've left if it wasn't something...well something as tragic as this."

"I just couldn't stay after I found out."

"I wish you told me."

"I wanted to tell you, but there was no way to do it

without hurting you more. Because not only did he cheat again, now I'm your—"

"*Don't*. Please don't say it out loud."

We both fell silent. I pinched the area between my thumb and index finger, hoping this was a nightmare that I could wake up from. It wasn't.

As time passed, I knew there was nothing else to say.

There was no more us.

There never could be.

I needed to get up. I needed to be alone with my thoughts. I needed to crawl into a ball and sleep for a very long time. But I couldn't make myself leave that cold bathroom floor beside the guy who broke my heart without ever meaning to.

"I miss you," Crew said.

"I'm right here," I said.

"Yeah, but you feel miles away now."

A million miles away.

"What do we do now?" he asked.

"Find a good therapist?"

Silent laughter escaped us. It was all we could do to stop from being leveled by the weight of our new reality.

"I'm not sure your mother knows..." he said.

My mother. My *poor* mother.

"Are you going to tell her?" he asked.

I shrugged. "I think I need to wrap my head around it first."

"*Fuuuuuuck*," Crew roared, dropping his head back against the wall we leaned on.

I had the same urge to curse the universe that was currently having a field day with us. Why couldn't we have just stayed enemies? "Have you talked to your mom since you found out?"

He shook his head. "I needed to be away from her. She'd kept that from me my whole life. Even this summer, when she *knew* I was staying at his house, she said *nothing*."

"Did you talk to my—" I winced. "*Our* father?"

"Don't call him that. A father doesn't pay a woman to get rid of his kid."

I met his eyes. "He did that?"

Crew nodded. "He was furious when he found out about me. He asked her what she used the money for."

Tears slipped from my eyes. "I'm glad she didn't do it."

Crew lifted his thumb and wiped away my tears. "Me too."

It was wrong of me to rely on him for comfort. But I couldn't not let him do it. I needed him to. "This sucks."

"That's one word for it," he agreed.

Not wanting to prolong the inevitable, I stood on shaky legs. "I should go."

Crew stood and followed me to the exit. As soon as we got outside, I knew I'd need to say goodbye to him. To what we'd once been. To my short bout of happiness.

I grasped the doorknob.

"It was real," Crew said.

I paused.

"Everything between us," he explained. "It was all real."

Tears glazed my eyes. And, despite every part of my body yearning to stay there with him, I opened the door and walked out. I prayed my wobbly legs would not give out on me as I made my way toward the parking lot in the darkness.

Once I was inside Gina's car, I dropped my head to the steering wheel and sobs tore out of me.

CHAPTER TWENTY-EIGHT

ot wanting to answer a bunch of questions I couldn't even wrap my own head around, I left Gina's car keys on her doorstep. I hurried to my house and entered the kitchen through the back door. There was a note on the island.

In Boston for the weekend.

Coward.

He didn't even have the balls to tell me the truth when I begged him to tell me what happened. He let me walk around for days not knowing where Crew went and why he left. And, all along, he knew the truth.

I climbed the steps to the second floor and entered my room. I eyed my bed, but decided on some fresh air. I moved to my French doors and pulled them open. I stepped onto my balcony and sat in my new Adirondack chair. I rested my head back and stared up at the stars, trying not to think of my night under the stars on the island with Crew. But it was all I could think about. How happy I'd been. How happy he'd been.

A shooting star moved across the sky, and I laughed. Of course I'd see a shooting star right now. Crew harassed me for not wishing on things, so I made a wish—for all of this to be a dream.

I closed my eyes and listened to the crashing of the waves. If I could just focus on them, my mind wouldn't take me to places I didn't want it to go. I needed to release my anger at my father. I needed to forget my feelings for Crew. I needed to focus on being happy.

Tears snuck out of my closed eyes.

The truth remained. None of those options were possible. Because none of those options put Crew and me together at the end.

———

"Peyton!" Gina called.

Still curled in a ball on my Adirondack chair, I cracked open my eyes, happy to see the sun wasn't shining.

"Where are you?" she called from my patio down below.

"Up here," I grumbled. The overcast sky would make it easier to stay out there.

Within seconds, she was on my balcony. "You haven't answered your phone all night. What happened?"

"Nothing you could ever even imagine," I assured her.

"What's that mean?" she asked, crouching beside me.

"It's over."

"What? Why?"

I shifted in my chair so I was sitting on my ass and not my hip. "Because it just won't work."

"Says who?"

"Both of us. We agreed we're better off as friends."

She stood up and leaned against the railing with crossed arms. "I don't understand."

"Can we not talk about it right now?"

"Of course we need to talk about it. The guy packed up and disappeared leaving you heartbroken. Now, you're telling me he reappears and you decide you're better off as friends. What am I missing?"

I shrugged.

"Did he hurt you?" Gina pressed.

"No."

"Did he cheat?" she asked.

I shook my head.

"Is he going to jail?"

My brows furrowed and I shook my head.

"Did you find out he killed someone?"

I shook my head.

"What else could it be? Are you guys related?"

I stared at her, physically unable to admit that she'd guessed this unfathomable truth.

I don't think Gina's eyes could've grown any bigger as she grasped the significance of my silence.

"I don't even know what to say," she said.

"There's nothing to say."

"When you say related..."

I closed my eyes and tears escaped them.

Gina climbed into my lap, dropping her head onto my shoulder. "Oh, Peyton."

"I know. It's sick," I said, knowing what she was thinking.

"You didn't know," she assured me.

"You have to promise me you won't tell anyone," I pleaded. "Not Cody. Not your parents."

Gina made a cross over her heart with her finger. "Promise."

We stayed silent as the waves crashed in the background and Gina processed what I'd told her—as if that would ever even be possible.

CHAPTER TWENTY-NINE

"Thank you for seeing me," I said as I looked around the small office. A small waterfall that was meant to sound peaceful and soothing sat on the single shelf, and the table to my right held a basket filled with fidgets and a box of tissues.

"It's my pleasure," Blythe, the therapist seated across from me, said. "Gina demanded that I take you in today."

I laughed. "She's a good friend."

"And a great niece. So, where would you like to begin?" Blythe asked, pushing her rectangular glasses up from the tip of her nose where they kept slipping to.

"I've been having panic attacks for a year."

"That must be very scary," she said.

I shrugged.

"Do you know what triggers them?"

"Situations that feel out of my control," I explained.

"And do you often feel that you're placed in situations that are out of your control?"

"This year? Yes. Before that, I thought I had the perfect life."

"Well, panic attacks are the body's way of handling those situations. Fight or flight. Do you remember what caused the first one?"

"What I say here is confidential, right?" I asked.

She nodded. "Unless I'm worried for your safety or the safety of others."

"I understand," I said, noticing a painting on the wall of a woman alone on a beach holding her hat to her head, as if the wind would take it if she didn't. I couldn't help but see the parallel to my life. On the beach, I was at peace, but something kept happening to try to steal away my happiness.

"So, you were going to tell me what caused the first panic attack," she prompted.

I looked back to her. "I found out my father had an affair and fathered a child."

"That's some pretty heavy stuff," she said.

"It's bullshit," I said matter-of-factly.

"How have you been handling the attacks?"

"I breathe."

"Breathing's very important. Does it always work?"

I shrugged. "Eventually."

"Well, just know, that won't always work. Sometimes the attacks are more intense than you can handle with simply breathing."

"Yeah, that's why I'm here. I have a feeling worse ones are yet to come."

"Why do you say that?" she asked.

"I just found out my father cheated with another woman and fathered another child."

"Oh," she said.

"And..." I grabbed a fidget and toyed with the buttons on the square gadget.

"Go on," she prompted.

"The child I just found out about..." I pressed the buttons on the fidget, unable to say the words aloud.

"Take your time," she offered.

"It turns out that child is my boyfriend—well ex-boyfriend now."

She blinked hard, though she recovered quickly. "That would certainly cause more intense attacks. But you seem to be dealing right now."

"I'm good at faking it," I said.

She grinned. "Aren't we all? But, truthfully, tell me how you're feeling about what you just discovered."

"Truthfully?"

She nodded.

"I want to scream until I lose my voice. I want to hit something with a bat until I can't swing it any longer. I want my father out of my life forever. And, I want this all to be a vicious joke."

"Those are normal feelings when we're grieving."

"How can I be grieving if no one died?"

"Losing someone in a tragic way like you did is like death. You go through all the same emotions. Denial is the first stage of grief. You wanting it to be a joke is you wanting to deny that this is unfortunately your new reality. Anger is the second stage. You wanting to hit something or scream—rightfully so—fits that stage."

"So, if I go through all the stages, will I still have my panic attacks?"

"I don't know. But, you sought me out. Therapy is a great first step. Have you considered medication?" she asked.

"I don't want to be medicated."

"That *is* your choice. But just know there's nothing

wrong with using medication to help with something that's out of your control. There are many options out there—some stronger than others."

I shook my head. "I don't want to go that route."

"Then you won't. Let's discuss other techniques then."

———

My headlights led the way as I picked up Gina in my mom's Jeep and drove to the next town over.

"Just tell me where we're going?" she asked, staring out the window at the passing restaurants and stores.

"Nope."

"Are we meeting anyone there?"

"Nope."

"And you said this was my aunt's suggestion?"

"Yup." I flipped on my blinker and pulled into a parking lot.

Gina read the big neon sign. "Smash Zone?" She looked to me confused.

"You ready to break stuff?"

Once we were in our one-piece jumpsuits, helmets with face shields, ear covers, and gloves, we were led into a dark room lit only with black lights making the graffiti on the walls glow. The worker pointed to the rack of weapons we could choose from: a hammer, sledgehammer, bat, crowbar, metal pipe. I grabbed the bat and Gina grabbed the hammer.

"Once the music begins, you can start smashing," he said to me. He glanced to Gina who seemed completely out of her element assessing the bottles, mannequins, mirrors, tires, and windows that we could rage out on. "Just make sure your friend is nowhere near you when you begin," he instructed me.

I laughed to myself as he stepped out of the room. I looked around at the many smashable items, and my body itched to begin.

A few seconds later, heavy metal music blared into the room.

"Ready?" I yelled to Gina.

She shrug-nodded.

I swung the bat with everything I had at the bottles dangling from ropes from the ceiling. They smashed instantly. Gina lifted her arms over her head to protect herself from flying glass, even though the protective gear wouldn't let anything hurt her.

I turned to a nearby window propped up on the floor. I swung the bat, smashing all the glass panes.

I looked to Gina. "Hit something!" I yelled over the music.

She turned to a mirror and hit it with her hammer. It made a small spiderweb fissure.

"Swing harder!" I yelled.

She did, winding up and smashing the mirror completely. She spun to look at me. "This is fun!" she yelled.

I laughed.

We spent the next half an hour making sure that not a single smashable item in the room was left un-smashed. It felt so damn good to break things. To get my anger out. To feel free. I needed the release more than I realized.

CHAPTER THIRTY

"You've got this," Gina said as we pulled into the parking lot of the baseball field on Saturday night.

I didn't want to be there. I couldn't think of a worse place to be. But Blythe told me I needed to keep living. I couldn't hide or the panic attacks could intensify. I also couldn't let Gina down; she wanted me by her side for the championship game. I hadn't seen Crew since our talk in the field house, and I dreaded the moment our eyes locked. But it was inevitable. Whether it happened on the Cape or in Alabama, I knew we'd see each other again.

We parked and walked out to our spot on the first base line, opening our chairs and sitting down amongst more fans than we'd seen all season. I looked out at the field. Crew played catch with Sam. He smiled at something Sam said, and it was good to know he was no longer worried about telling me the truth. I knew that had weighed on him. But I couldn't help but wonder if he was feeling like me or if he was already over me given that our fate was decided for us.

Sam caught sight of me, and he waved before throwing

the ball to Crew. Crew turned to look and when he saw me, he shot me a sad smile. I gave him a quick wave and looked to Gina, releasing the breath I'd been holding.

"You're good," Gina assured me.

I closed my eyes, keeping the tears at bay. This was not going to be easy. There'd be no little leaguer bringing me baseballs. There'd be no home runs hit on my account. There would be girls trying to catch his eye. But he was no longer a guy I had any right to be jealous over.

By the bottom of the fifth inning, the Sharks and Stone Crabs were tied at two. Crew walked up to the batter's box. The girls behind us screamed his name, and he glanced in our direction. I quickly averted my gaze so not to catch his eyes.

In the batter's box, Crew got into his stance. The Stone Crabs' pitcher wound up, delivering a perfect fastball. Crew swung and connected, sending the ball flying high to left field and right over the fence.

The crowd around me jumped up, cheering his home run as the Sharks took the lead.

Crew kept his head down as he circled the bases, only to be bombarded by his teammates once he stepped on home plate. I caught a smile on his face as his teammates walked him back to the dugout.

By the bottom of the ninth, they were tied again. Cody was first up to bat.

"Let's go, Cody!" Gina yelled, taking me by surprise.

"Look at you getting into the game," I said.

"It's more like letting all these girls know he's taken," she whispered.

I laughed as Cody stepped into the batter's box. The Stone Crabs' pitcher wound up and delivered a high fastball. Cody ignored it. He stepped out of the box and took a minute then stepped back in. The pitcher shook off his catcher's sign and nodded at the next. He wound up and delivered a sinker. Cody again ignored it and the crowd cheered at the 2 and o count. The pitcher again shook off his catcher's sign, nodding at the next. He wound up and released the pitch. Cody swung. The bat connected. The ball soared. Everyone jumped to their feet watching as the ball sailed over the right fielder's head and over the fence.

Gina jumped up and down as the crowd around us went wild. Cody circled the bases to the applause of hundreds. When he approached home plate, his teammates were surrounding it. He jumped into the air and landed with both feet on the plate. His teammates celebrated around him, banging his helmet and hugging each other—the perfect end to an ideal summer for them.

At the brief trophy ceremony, Cody was awarded the game's MVP trophy. He stood at home plate and lifted it above his head. I clapped while Gina recorded the whole ceremony on her phone.

Once the ceremony ended and the crowd began to disperse, I stayed at my seat as Gina ran down to the fence, waiting for Cody to walk off the field. As soon as he did, she launched herself into his arms. A tinge of jealousy swirled in my gut, knowing that would have been Crew and me just a week ago.

Breathe.

I stood up and closed our chairs, reminding myself that it wasn't my reality anymore.

Breathe.

I scooped up the chairs and made my way toward the exit. I did a good job sitting through the whole game when I didn't think I'd be able to.

Small victories.

I waited in the car for Gina, scanning my newsfeed on my phone. Gina eventually slipped into the driver's seat.

"Was he happy?" I asked, already knowing the answer.

"He was on cloud nine. We're gonna continue the party at Monty's."

"Would you mind dropping me at home?" I asked.

"I'm not gonna beg you to go. But please know I want to celebrate with you too. You've been there since Cody and I first met. This is a big night for him, and I want both of us to be there for him."

I inhaled a deep breath.

"But I'm your best friend," she continued, "and I would never force you to do something you didn't want to do."

We both burst out in laughter.

"Okay. Okay," she said. "I always force you to do things you don't want to do, but I want you by my side. And I don't want you to regret missing out on fun things because you expect them to suck."

"How long do you plan on staying?" I asked.

"Is that a yes?"

"I'll make an appearance," I said, earning myself a giant smile from Gina.

We arrived at Monty's and, between tourists, Sharks fans, and players, the place was packed. The music's bass pumped through the room like its very own heartbeat as we weaved our way through groups of people to the bar.

Gina grabbed us each a beer, and we maneuvered ourselves through the crowd until we reached the back patio. As soon as we stepped outside, we spotted Cody doing shots at the tiki bar with some of his teammates. His arms lifted into the air, and he howled when he spotted Gina. She glanced to me with wide eyes knowing this was going to be a sloppy night for Cody. Still, she made her way to him, and he wrapped her in a giant hug.

"There she is!"

I turned toward the voice. Sam was standing there. "Congratulations," I said.

"Thanks," he said.

"The season's over. Does that mean our summer bromance is over too?" I asked, sipping my beer.

He smirked. "It doesn't have to be."

"We'll always have the Cape, Sam," I said dramatically.

He laughed.

I spotted Gina who was looking behind me with wide eyes. I glanced over my shoulder, immediately locking eyes with Crew. My heart started racing. It sucked being attracted to a guy I could never have. But, I couldn't just shut off my feelings for him. They didn't just disappear now that I wasn't allowed to be attracted to him.

But what were we to each other now?

Friends? Acquaintances? Siblings?

A pretty girl stepped up to him, pulling his attention away from me.

Knots twisted in my stomach as I watched him smile at her the same way he used to smile at me. The imaginary weight pressed against my chest. The suffocating feeling sucked away my air. I clutched a nearby table as I gasped for air.

"Peyton?" Sam said moving to my side.

Breathe.

"Are you okay?" he asked.

Breathe.

I nodded.

"I don't believe you."

"I need to go home," I managed.

"I'm taking you," he said, linking his arm through mine.

"I don't want you to leave your celebration," I said as we moved away from the patio.

"I'll come back," he assured me.

Sam had me home within minutes, and thankfully my attack subsided, leaving me with a dull ache in my chest and a splitting headache. And, though I argued, Sam walked me to my front door.

"Thanks for everything," I said before hugging him.

"You make it easy."

"Said no person ever," I said as I stepped out of the hug.

"Do you want me to help you get inside?" he asked.

"I'm fine." I opened the door and stepped inside, turning back to him. "Don't even think about forgetting me once you're rich and famous."

He smiled. "How could I ever?"

I smiled and closed the door, grateful to have met people like Sam this summer. I guess not all ball players were trouble.

CHAPTER THIRTY-ONE

I walked upstairs, knowing I needed to sleep off the effects of the panic attack. I brushed my teeth, washed my face, and pulled my hair into a messy bun. I slipped on my pajamas and climbed into bed. Between the attack and my emotions being so out of whack, as soon as I closed my eyes, I felt myself drifting off.

There was a soft knock on my bedroom door.

I opened my eyes, but my room was still dark. I couldn't be sure if I'd dreamt the sound or if it was just my imagination running wild. I closed my eyes, trying to fall back asleep, but there was another knock.

My eyes popped open. I knew I locked my bedroom door, but I was home alone. No one should've been knocking on my bedroom door. I grabbed my phone and dialed nine-one-one but didn't hit *send*. I slipped out from under my covers and moved to my chair, grabbing the bottle of pepper spray that I kept for an emergency in my handbag. I held my finger on the nozzle of the pepper spray, switched on my bedroom light, then cracked open the door.

I inhaled sharply.

Crew stood there with his hands in his pockets.

I lowered the pepper spray and opened the door the rest of the way. "What are you doing here?"

"I just wanted to see if you were okay," he said.

"I'm good," I lied.

He eyed the pepper spray in my hand. "Did I scare you?"

"Of course you scared me. I'm home alone and someone's knocking on my bedroom door."

"Sorry."

I huffed. "It's fine." I stepped aside so he could come in.

"You sure?" he asked.

"Who the hell knows anymore," I said as he moved past me into my room and I closed the door.

His body felt so much bigger in my room now that we were alone...and not together anymore. His eyes swept around, taking in my unmade bed. "Did I wake you?"

"Not really," I said, turning off my phone and tucking the pepper spray back into my handbag.

He leaned against my dresser with his hands in his pockets. "I'm glad you came to the game."

"Yeah?" I asked as I sat down on the edge of my bed.

He nodded, and the awkwardness in the room was enough to drive a sane person crazy.

"Well, congratulations. You guys deserved to win."

"Cody really came through," he said.

"Yeah. I'm so happy for him."

"Did Sam bring you home?" Crew asked.

"Yeah. Didn't he make it back to Monty's?"

He shrugged.

"Oh, you might've been too busy with that girl to notice," I said, trying not to sound jealous even though I selfishly was.

"She was nobody," he said.

I held up my hands, wishing I wasn't relieved to hear that. "Not my business."

"Of course it's your business." He pushed off my dresser and walked the few feet to my bed, sitting down beside me. His weight dipped the bed pulling me closer to him, but I stopped myself from leaning into him. "I can't stand this distance between us."

I looked down, suddenly scared to be that close to him.

"This week's been hell," he began. "All I kept seeing was the look on your face when I told you why I left."

"I'm fine."

"Well, I'm far from it."

My eyes lifted to his. "I think we need to consider what happened between us as a blip in time," I said. "We had no idea we were...you know...so it didn't really count."

"It's not just that, Peyton," he said, pain evident in his features. "It's the fact that I can't shake you."

My eyes widened, blindsided by his admission.

"I miss the feel of your skin," he continued. "The taste of your kiss. Your laugh—"

"Stop," I whispered.

"I don't care who you are," he continued. "I just want to be with you."

"Stop," I repeated as my heart began to thrash against the wall of my chest.

"Why?"

I wanted him to want me as much as I wanted him to stay away from me. That's what made it so difficult. The conflicting feelings were at constant odds with each other. But in the end, we needed to forget everything that happened. "Because we can't."

"Says who?"

I swallowed down the lump of emotion in my throat. "Crew."

"Peyton."

"Don't make this any harder than it already is," I said.

"Harder? You just said you were fine," he reminded me.

"Well—"

His lips crashed against mine. I pressed my hands to his chest to push him back, but he slipped his arms around me, holding me tightly to him.

This is wrong.

This is so wrong.

But I couldn't stop. Our tongues moved together like they had so many times before. I was home in his arms. I was *his* in his arms. And despite the truth, I wanted to forget it all for the night and get lost in his kiss.

But I couldn't.

I pulled back, breathless and flushed. "We can't do this."

"We just did," he countered.

"Well, it can't happen again," I said, trying to get my heart and head in sync.

He swept a loose strand of my hair away from my face, and his touch elicited tingles to my skin. "Let me stay with you tonight."

"No."

"You're in this big house alone. I'd feel better if I stayed."

"I told you I'm fine."

"I promise I won't do anything like we just did," he said.

"*You* just did. *I* was an unwilling participant."

He scoffed, not buying a word of it. "There's nothing wrong with us sharing a bed if we're fully clothed. We did it many times."

"You have your own house," I said, knowing this was a terrible idea. "And, your own bed."

He paused for a long moment, and I expected him to agree to leave. "Yeah, but my heart's here."

A shiver racked through my body.

"And, I don't fucking know what to do with that."

My stomach flipped over. He couldn't say things like that and make me feel things I shouldn't feel.

He cupped my cheeks between his hands and stared into my eyes. "We're in this together. We're the only ones who understand what the other's going through."

My eyes riveted between his. He was right. We were alone in this. No one else could possibly understand. And, although I knew the difference between right and wrong, I just wasn't strong enough to force him away.

I pulled away from his hands, inching back toward my pillow. Crew realized what I was doing and stood up. I slipped under my covers.

Taking this as me acquiescing, he shucked his sneakers and peeled his shirt over his head. That's when I saw he was wearing my pink shell necklace.

I sucked in a sharp breath and tears stung my eyes.

He switched off my lights, and then we were in complete darkness. He walked to my bed and climbed under the blankets, spooning me like he had many times before. And, I didn't even fight it.

We lay in silence.

I focused on the soft whoosh of our breaths and the steady thuds of our heartbeats. I tried not to focus on the way his hard body pressed to mine. Or, the way his arms wrapped around my body so that we fit perfectly together. I tried not to inhale his sandalwood scent which was wrapped around me like a lost blanket that I'd just found again.

"You took my necklace," I said.

"I needed to have a piece of you with me."

I didn't know how to respond.

"We wasted a lot of time," he said.

"You were a stubborn ass."

He laughed. "Takes one to know one."

"Hindsight," I mused.

"I still can't believe you let me sleep in bed with you that first night."

"Why?"

"I thought for sure you were plotting something."

I laughed. "Yeah, I'm quite sneaky like that."

"Well, you and Gina pulled off a good one with your wigs. Even if I wasn't fooled."

"How did you know?" I asked.

"When you only have eyes for one person, you notice everything about them. The way they walk. The way they hold their head. The curves of their body. I spotted you the second you sat down in those right field bleachers."

A strange combination of sadness and joy swirled low in my belly. How could I feel both at the same time? It was so strange to be so close yet so far away from another human being—especially one you shared memories with. "This isn't making things easier."

"What?" he asked.

"It's easier to get over someone you don't see."

"I don't want you to get over me," he said.

"That's not fair."

"Why not?" he asked.

"Don't you want me to be happy?"

"Yeah, with me."

"*Crew*."

"It's not like our parents are together."

"Do you even hear yourself right now?"

"Yeah. Who's ever gonna know if we don't say anything?"

"I'll know," I challenged.

"Does it make you sick knowing we...?"

"I don't want to regret it, but, now that we know, I know it's wrong."

He didn't respond.

Did he seriously think if no one knew, we could carry on like we didn't share DNA? Was it that easy for him to overlook it? "This was a bad idea," I said, attempting to get out of his arms.

He tightened his arms around me. "I won't say anything else. Just please don't take this away from me."

Tears pricked my eyes. I knew, when he left in the morning, I'd need to stay away from him. I'd never get over him if all I could see was him.

CHAPTER THIRTY-TWO

"Ohmigod!"

Crew and I jumped up, blinded by the sunlight filling my room.

Gina stood in the doorway glaring at us. "What's this?" she said, her hand shooting out at us in my bed.

I pressed my palms to my eyes, pushing sleep away. "It's nothing."

Crew's eyes cut to mine. "Nothing?"

"You shouldn't be here like...this," Gina said.

"You told her?" he asked me.

"I had to tell someone."

Crew threw off the covers and sat on the edge of my bed.

"And since Peyton's too nice to send you away, I think I need to do it for her," Gina said.

"I said he could stay," I explained. "We had a lot to talk about."

"Then why's he shirtless?" she asked.

"I'm shirtless," Crew began, "because I was sleeping."

She crossed her arms. "Exes shouldn't be sleeping shirt-less *or* in the same bed."

The word exes turned my stomach. We were so much more than that. And it hurt. It hurt like fucking hell. "We slept in bed together when we hated each other," I explained. "This was no big deal."

Crew stood up and grabbed his shirt from my chair a little more aggressively than necessary making me think calling it no big deal hurt him. He pulled the shirt over his head then slipped on his shoes. His eyes locked on mine. "I meant every word I said last night."

My eyes lowered, unable to look at him.

"You know where I'm staying," he said as he walked to the door.

I glanced up in time to see him stop. I thought he'd turn and say something else, but he didn't. He walked out.

Gina rushed over and sat beside me. "Why did he come over?"

"Because we're the only ones who know how it feels."

"I wish I could make it all better," she said.

"Me too." I fell back onto my bed. "It'd help if my feelings for him would just go away."

"Oh, honey. How can you be expected to just switch off feelings?"

"Especially when he says he wants us to stay together because we don't have the same mother."

"*Wow*," Gina said. "He's got it bad."

"It can't happen," I said.

"I'll support whatever you choose to do," Gina said.

"There's no choice," I said. "It's over."

———

"I'd finally let down my guard with someone. I finally trusted a ball player. And what did it get me? The rug ripped out from under me and a broken heart," I said, playing with the squishy ball I'd grabbed from the fidget basket.

"Tell me how you felt when he was saying all of those things to you," Blythe said.

"Hopeful. Which I know is crazy."

"There's nothing wrong with feeling hopeful. But I will say I'm concerned with what you'll do with your feelings when hope runs out."

I said nothing, knowing the hope I felt was momentary and reality had quickly set in.

"Let's talk about your father," she said, switching gears.

"Let's not."

"I think we can both agree he is the root of all the issues you're facing."

I didn't respond because it was the truth.

"Correct me if I'm wrong," she continued. "Your panic attacks began when the truth about his infidelity came to light."

I nodded.

"And they intensified being around him this summer."

I nodded.

"We need to address these unresolved feelings you have toward him."

"I hate him."

"But you didn't always. It's why your mom wanted you both under the same roof. She knew that you'd both have to finally address the issues. She couldn't have planned on his presence eliciting a physical reaction in you. But her intentions were good."

"All we do is fight," I said.

"Yes, but have you gotten the opportunity to say anything you were holding inside?"

I thought back to our interactions. I had definitely made my hate clear.

"If he were in front of you right now, what would you say to him?" she asked.

"You destroyed my life."

"That's a start. Anything else?"

"You're deceitful."

"Good."

"You don't care about anyone but yourself."

"Stop there. Can you think of a time when he did care about you?"

"Up until last summer, I felt it my entire life."

"Could all of that been deception?" she asked.

I shrugged, not wanting to admit there had been many good times with him.

"Might he have shielded you from his other life because when he was with you, it was all about you and not other women?"

I shrugged.

"If you don't mind me asking, up until last summer, how did he treat your mother?"

"The same way he treated me. Like she was the center of his universe. That's the hardest part. He never let on that he was this cheater living a whole other life."

"That would be hard to wrap your head around. So, what else would you say to him?"

"You need to be better for Crew."

She narrowed her eyes. "Better for Crew?"

"He can't keep running away from his mistakes. He needs to face them head on." I'd been so swept up in how his infidelity affected Crew and me as a couple, I hadn't considered that Crew was dealing with a separate issue when it came to knowing he had a father. My father couldn't just walk away from Crew like he had his other child. Crew deserved better.

"Maybe you need to tell him that."

CHAPTER THIRTY-THREE

As people shuffled in and out of the café, I stared down at my phone. Noon had come and gone, and it was nearing twelve-thirty. Either he was blowing me off, or he was making me wait the way I would've made him wait if it had been the other way around and he'd asked to see me in a public place.

The bell on the door jingled and my father finally strode inside pulling his sunglasses off his face. Many heads turned because that's what happened when Marty Richmond entered a building. Men whispered to their friends, and woman took photos on their phones.

He stepped up to my table, but I stayed where I was. He slipped into the seat across from me. "I'm surprised you wanted to meet me here."

"I needed witnesses in case you planned to lay another hand on me."

He huffed his frustration with me. "That was a mistake."

"Oh, good to see you're finally acknowledging your mistakes."

"When's this gonna end, Peyton?"

"When's what gonna end?"

He glanced around the café, likely making sure none of his adoring fans could hear our less-than-amicable conversation. "This animosity you've got toward me?"

I gave the obligatory moment to appear as if I was actually considering his question. "Probably never."

"Good to know." He grasped the arms of the chair, preparing to stand up. "Are we done then?"

"We deserved better. Mom and me. We held down the fort while you were off playing baseball, and you repaid us by cheating and having two other children—at least two that we know of."

He stayed in his seat but leaned in angrily. "I gave you the best of everything. I think you're forgetting that."

"All I ever wanted was to be loved. And to know the person who loved me—who brought me into this world—loved me and my family more than cheap nights with baseball whores."

He stared at me like I was someone he didn't even know. Had my words meant nothing?

"Have you ever even reached out to your other daughter?" I asked.

"Why would I?"

"Because she's an innocent bystander in all of this. So is Crew."

He balked.

"Are you gonna pretend he's not yours either? Or, because he's gonna be a big baseball star, do you now want him?"

"Watch it Peyton. I'm still your father."

"And Crew's the guy I fell in love with," I blurted.

His head cocked to the side. "Come again?"

"We were together this summer."

"Jesus Christ," he reproached. "What were you *thinking*?"

"What was *I* thinking? That's classic coming from you."

He shook his head as if he wasn't the cause of all of this.

"How would I *ever* know my father cheated on my mother with yet another woman and had yet another kid—oh, and this time the kid would end up living in my house? And, he'd end up being my age and athletic and charming and someone I fell for?"

"You're not to see him again," he ordered.

"Don't you think I know that? Don't you think I feel sick over what happened?"

The look of disgust on his face rubbed me the wrong way. I needed him to understand how his selfishness affected everyone around him. "I *still* love him. Imagine having to figure out what to do with those feelings. It's awesome."

He dragged in a deep breath, releasing it slowly. "I paid her a lot of money. I never could've imagined she would have kept the money *and* the kid." He shook his head as if disgusted by Crew's mother when he was the one who was disgusting. "I'm not even convinced he's mine," he said offhandedly.

A piercing sound rang out in my ears. "What?"

"She slept with a lot of players. Women like her are always looking for a payday and will do and say anything to get one. At the time, it was just easier to pay her to leave me alone."

"Are you saying you never asked for proof?"

"Why would I? I thought she was getting rid of it," he countered.

I couldn't believe my ears. "How about when she

showed up at the beach house? You didn't think to ask for a DNA test then?"

"I just wanted her gone."

I closed my eyes and pressed my palms to my forehead. "Jesus Christ."

"Look, I had no idea you and Crew even—"

"I need you to take a paternity test," I said, my head spinning with the possibilities. But I wouldn't give myself false hope. I couldn't afford to. I jumped up. "We're getting the test right now."

CHAPTER THIRTY-FOUR

I knocked on the front door of a small beach house with the paternity test in a bag in my hand. DePetrillo opened the door.

"Is Crew here?" I asked.

He pointed up to the stairs behind him.

"Thanks." I sprinted upstairs and knocked on the only closed door. When there was no answer, I opened it. Crew lay on the bed with headphones on and his eyes closed. Not wanting to startle him, I crept over and carefully lowered myself down on the edge of the bed. When he felt the bed dip, he opened his eyes and ripped off his headphones. "Hey," he said, visibly confused by my presence. "What are you doing here?"

"I saw my father today," I said.

"Okay," he said, waiting for me to elaborate.

"He said he wasn't sure you were his."

He sat up with wild eyes. "What?"

"He agreed to take a paternity test."

Crew looked at the bag in my hand.

"I need you to swab your cheek and in two days we'll

know."

"Jesus Christ," he said, his eyes full of wonder.

"I know. I'm trying not to get my hopes up." I pulled the box out of the bag. My father had already given me the swab sample. I just needed Crew's. I opened the box, pulled the swab from its wrapper, and handed it to him. "Just rub it around the inside of your cheek for about thirty seconds."

When Crew was done swabbing, he handed me the stick and I put it in the tube and closed it.

"Now what?" he asked.

"We send it off, and I'll get an email with the results in two days," I explained.

He stood up. "Come on. Let's get it to the post office."

On the short walk to the post office, every possible what-if played through my mind. What if the test proved he was my father's child? What if we remained in the same tragic situation?

But...

What if his mom was wrong?

Once we reached the post office, we requested overnight delivery. The postal worker assured us it would be there by noon the following day. I watched until she disappeared into the back room with the package, hoping the sooner it got to the lab, the sooner we'd have the results.

We started walking back toward DePetrillo's house.

"I'm scared," Crew said.

My eyes moved to his. "What are you scared of?"

"Letting myself believe there's a possibility I'll be able to hold you again."

I released a silent breath.

"It's like we've been given this second chance, but only maybe."

He was right. It was terrifying to let our minds even go there. "I've been going to counseling."

"Really?"

I nodded.

"And?"

"And, it's probably a good thing I'm talking to someone. I was holding too much in."

"I'm proud of you," he said.

"I didn't say I'm cured."

"But it's a step in the right direction," he acknowledged.

"Oh, and I almost forgot. I saw a shooting star the other night."

"Yeah? Did you make a childish wish?"

"I sure did."

He smiled, and I could see he was proud of me. "I hope it comes true."

"Me too," I agreed.

"Can I ask you something?" Crew asked.

"Sure."

"If this doesn't end the way we want it to, can you promise you won't shut me out. I want you in my life, no matter what."

He was asking for something I wasn't sure I could do. How would I ever be able to see him with another girl? How could I pretend to be happy for him? How could I just stop having feelings for him? I didn't know how to respond because our love story was hashtag tragic. But at least for the time being, we had hope. "I can try."

CHAPTER THIRTY-FIVE

I awoke the next day, immediately grabbing my phone to check my email. But like I already knew, the results weren't in yet. I tossed my phone down and climbed out of bed. I moved to my dresser, pulling open the top drawer.

I reached inside and pulled out a baseball, twisting it in my hand and reading the message: *Go Out With Me.* I closed my eyes and thought back to the moment Crew sent the little leaguer over to me. And, though I'd never admit it to him, it was adorable. No one had ever gone to such lengths to get my attention.

I reached back in the drawer and pulled out the other ball. I turned it in my palm and read the message: *Don't Move.* I closed my eyes and thought back to our night on the baseball field. Him thinking I wouldn't know how to play was hysterical. I'd grown up around baseball. How could he ever think he'd be able to teach *me* how to play the game?

I placed the balls back in the drawer—my own pieces of Crew—before I flopped back down on my bed. I grabbed my phone and opened a blank note and began to type:

Blissful, Beloved, Beautiful...
Baseball is.
Boastful, Bold, Brave...
Baseball players are.
Strong, Strategic, Showoffs...
Shortstops are.
Courageous, Captivating, Caring...
Crew is.

I opened my texts and typed: **I think I owe you a poem.** Then, I pasted the poem in and sent it to Crew.

I waited for what felt like forever. And then the bouncing dots appeared. **I love it**.

———

"I think you need to be optimistic," Blythe said. "But know that things might not end the way you want them to."

I nodded, playing with the mini magnetics in my hand. She was not telling me something I didn't already know.

"Now, where are you at with your father?" she asked. "He met you at the café *and* he took the test. Did you appreciate that?"

I shrugged.

"Do you think you'll ever be able to forgive him?" she asked.

"No."

"Can I ask why not?"

"Because I'll never be able to forget what he did."

"I didn't say you need to forget it," she said. "I asked if you'll be able to forgive him."

"Isn't it the same thing?" I asked.

"*Forgetting* means not remembering something. *Forgiving* means sparing yourself the emotional burden of something painful. It means releasing it from your body, your mind, your soul. Don't you want to release the anger you feel?"

"I smashed a ton of stuff," I explained.

"That's a momentary release of anger. The anger you're holding onto toward your father is within you. It's going to take more than just smashing things to release it."

"So what else can I do?"

"Well, for your own well-being, I think you need to start forgiving him," she said.

———

I sat on the beach the next day in a hoodie and cutoffs. Today was another overcast day, and the wind had begun to pick up. Since August was winding down, the hot days of summer were too. It was hard to believe so much had happened this summer. Over the span of a few months, I'd left for Europe but ended up back on the Cape—a place I never planned to return to again. But, strangely, it turned out to be the one place where I was meant to be.

My phone pinged, and an email alert appeared on the screen. I knew right away it was from the lab. Before I opened the email, I texted Crew to come over.

I stared at the email preview, but I couldn't bring myself to open it.

It was a crazy thing to know my fate would be determined by a single email. Right now, I still had hope. Once I saw the results, that feeling would all be gone, and it would be replaced by one of two emotions: elation or despair.

Unable to wait any longer, I clicked on the email and opened the pdf entitled *DNA Test Results*. There were three columns of numbers: the first was a bunch of letters and numbers; the second was titled *child* with a line of numbers beneath it; the third was titled *alleged father* with another line of numbers beneath it. I had no idea what it all meant, but down below was a box entitled *interpretation*.

I made it bigger, reading the interpretation. "The alleged father..." I swallowed hard. "...is excluded as the biological father of the tested child..."

I couldn't even finish reading it because tears welled in my eyes. I fell back on the sand and squealed as a rush of emotions flooded me. Relief filled my mind, happiness swelled in my chest, and excitement overflowed in my heart.

Knowing Crew would be there soon, I stood up and jogged to the house. I entered the kitchen through the patio door and stopped short. My father sat at the island. I don't know what came over me—maybe Blythe's words or maybe the results on my phone—but I stepped up beside him.

He jumped, startled by my presence. "I didn't see you there."

"I forgive you," I said, a huge weight lifting from my shoulders once the words left my lips.

"You do?" he asked.

"I don't want to carry this hate in me anymore."

"I'm glad," he said.

"I want to trust people again and not expect the worst from everyone. I hated baseball players because of you."

"Not all ball players are untrustworthy."

I knew that. Crew taught me.

"So, what does this mean for us?" he asked.

"It means, I want Mom to be happy. I want you to go your separate ways for good. You're not the man she married, and I think you know that. She doesn't deserve to be in a marriage where she can't trust her husband."

"You're right."

"We're gonna be okay," I assured him.

"You and Mom or you and me?" he asked.

"Mom and I will definitely be okay. You and me will take some time. I need to get used to the idea that you're not the man I thought you were. Maybe that's on me. But it's gonna take time to get used to the man you are."

He nodded, as if what I'd said made sense to him. "I'm sorry I let you down."

"It was never about me." I turned away from him, knowing I'd been as honest as I could, and my snarky-ness was bound to rear its ugly head if I didn't walk away.

I hurried upstairs and entered my empty room. I sat on my bed with my phone in my hand and my heartbeat racing.

"Did you read it yet?" Crew asked as he entered my room.

I kept a straight face and nodded.

"What'd it say?"

I called up the pdf and tossed him my phone.

He caught it and stared down at the screen. I fought to conceal my smile as he read the news I already knew. When his eyes lifted to mine, a huge smile spread across his face. I stood up, and he wrapped me in his arms, squeezing me like I'd disappear if he didn't. "Thank God," he said, pressing kisses all over my head. "Thank God," he kept repeating.

"It's real," I said.

He pulled back so he could see my face. "It's always been real."

Stupid tears pricked my eyes again.

"I love you so damn much," he said before his lips

crashed to mine, kissing me the way I needed to be kissed—with so much love and relief. We had a future. Crew picked me up and carried me to my bed, lowering me to it without stopping kissing me.

I eventually needed to catch my breath, so I pulled back leaving us both gasping for air. "I never thought we'd get to do that again," I said.

"Careful. I might start thinking you only want me for one thing," he said.

"Oh, that's one of the things I want you for," I said.

He pressed a trail of kisses down my neck.

"What do you want *me* for?" I asked.

"Well, more poetry for starters."

I arched my neck, giving him better access.

"And, I want you at my games in a pink wig so I can see you at all times."

I laughed.

"And, I want you beside me when I find out if I make it to the big leagues next summer," he said, nibbling my ear.

"*When* you make it," I said. "Not *if*."

"You're my lucky charm," he said. "And I don't think I can be without you."

I rolled my eyes. "You're such a liar."

He pulled back and met my eyes. "I won't lie to you, Peyton. Not ever. You never have to worry about that."

A tear slipped down my cheek, the emotional day definitely catching up with me.

"And, I'll never hurt you." He patted his hand to his heart. "You worked your way in here the second you threw that chair off the balcony, and there's no going back from that."

My heart was a jackhammer in my chest.

"I've been on the receiving end of your hate, indifference, and love," he continued. "I'll take love any day of the week."

I tipped my head. "Love? Did I say love?"

He leaned forward and whispered, "I know you love me."

I stifled a smile. "You sure you're ready for all of me—the good, the bad, and the crazy?"

He laughed. "I wouldn't have it any other way."

I stared into his blue eyes, positive I could get lost in them forever.

"Are we gonna tell your dad?" he asked.

I shook my head. "Nope. We're gonna head downstairs, and we're gonna make out in front of him."

Crew laughed. "I think that's an awesome plan. The problem is, tonight, the only plan I have involves you, me, and this bed. Scaring the shit out of your father's gonna have to wait." And then he kissed me. And, he didn't stop kissing me. Or loving me. Or telling me what I wanted to hear...the truth. The good, the bad, and the ugly truth.

And I *loved* him for it.

Crew and I sat on the sofa in the beach house living room. We'd been on the Cape since graduating in May, and tonight was the night Crew had been waiting for since he was a kid.

"Is it on yet?" my mom asked, carrying a platter of food into the room where the flat screen aired the pre-draft commentary.

"Not yet," Gina said as Cody adjusted the laptop facing the sofa. Crew's reaction to wherever he went in the draft was being live-streamed.

Crew's knee bounced slightly. And even though he told his college teammates and his Sharks teammates who were there supporting him that he wasn't nervous, I could tell that he was.

"Am I late?" Crew's mom asked as she hurried into the house with a platter of cookies.

"Right on time," I assured her.

She placed her cookies down on the table, then moved to Crew's other side and sat down.

"It's starting," Sam said as the commissioner of baseball

appeared on the screen. He stood at a podium with a draft banner behind him and welcomed everyone to the draft. The crowd at the event in Seattle cheered.

Crew slipped his hand into mine, linking our fingers.

"Take a deep breath," I whispered, knowing there was definitely something to be said for breathing.

Everyone in the room grew silent.

On the television, the commissioner announced, "With the first pick in this year's major league draft, the Florida Marlins select Crew Burke, a shortstop from the University of Alabama."

The room around us exploded with cheers. Crew remained still as his mother hugged him. Then, he turned to me with excitement in his eyes and wrapped his arms around me.

"You deserve this," I whispered.

His teammates crowded around him, patting him on the back.

"They're waiting in Seattle," Crew's agent said as he fist-bumped Crew. "You ready?"

Crew nodded and his agent clicked something on the laptop. Instantly, the view of our living room was on the television screen.

"Crew. Congratulations," the sports announcer at the draft said.

"Thank you," Crew said.

"What's it feel like to go first in this year's draft?"

"It's surreal. It's a moment I've wished for my entire life." He bumped my leg gently at the mention of *wishing*.

"The Marlins could really use your bat in their lineup," the announcer said.

"I'm ready for any job they see fit for me. If it's my bat

they need, they've got it. If it's my glove in the field, they've got that too."

"You ready for Florida weather?" the announcer asked.

"I'm ready to play ball. It's a dream come true to be able to do it for my job, and I can't wait to bring my mom and my girlfriend along for the exciting ride."

"Crew Burke, we can't wait to see you play," the announcer said before the interview ended, and our living room was no longer on the television.

"Now, we can really party," Cody announced, and everyone in the room broke into laughter.

Crew stood from the sofa and grabbed my hand, pulling me to my feet. "Come with me."

We moved through the crowded living room, stopping every few feet so people could congratulate him. We eventually made it outside, and Crew led me across the back patio.

"Where are we going?" I asked.

He didn't answer; he just led me to the pool house. He pushed open the door and stepped inside. I followed him in, freezing when I saw what he'd done. Huge vases of flowers filled the pool house. Without releasing my hand, Crew stepped in front of me.

"This is the happiest day of my life," he began. "I got drafted with you by my side, and you agreed to spend the rest of your life with me."

I cocked my head. "That didn't happen."

He smirked before reaching into his back pocket and pulling out a diamond ring.

My heartbeat sped up as Crew dropped to one knee and held up the ring. The diamond sparkled like crazy under the skylights making it difficult to see anything else. "I'll tell you again what I told you last summer. When you're around, I'm incapable of seeing anyone but you. Because of you, I'm no longer the player you thought I was. Because of you, I'm so damn happy. So, marry me, Peyton. Be my lifelong teammate."

Heat pulsed in my cheeks as I stared at him kneeling in front of me.

"What do you say? Will you make another one of my wishes come true today?" he asked.

I thought about a life with Crew. All those away games. All those nights apart. All those video calls. Then, I did the only thing I could in that moment. I shook my head.

Fear shone in his eyes.

"This is *my* wish," I said. "Don't think you're gonna claim it."

He laughed, his fear morphing into hope.

"Thank you for making it come true," I continued. "Of course I'll marry you."

Crew's smile grew as he slipped the ring onto my finger.

I laughed as he scooped me up in his arms.

"I love you so much," he said, though he didn't let me respond because his lips captured mine.

"I love you two together!" Gina called through the door.

We pulled apart and turned toward the door. Gina, my mom, and Crew's mom stood outside the door smiling.

"I love us too!" I called, holding out my hand so they could see the ring.

Crew moved us to the door. I thought he was letting them in to celebrate, but instead, he closed the curtains so they couldn't see inside. Then he looked to me. "Now where were we?"

ALSO BY J. NATHAN

For You Sports Series:
Book #1 *For Finlay*
Book #2 *For Forester*
Book #3 *For Crosby*
Book #4 *For Emery*
Savage Beasts Rock Star Series:
Book #1 *Kozart*
Book #2 *Treyton*
Standalones:
All Your Tomorrows
Seren
Something About You
I Just Need You
You're the Reason
Until Alex
Before Hadley
Since Drew

ACKNOWLEDGMENTS

Thank you so much for taking the time to read Peyton and Crew's story. I hope you enjoyed it as much as I enjoyed writing it!

To all the influencers and readers who have shared my books. I could never do this without you! Thank you for taking *your* time to read, review, and share my books!

To my wonderful ARC team who read and reviewed *The Trouble with Players*. Thank you for always showing up for me when I need you the most. It means everything to me!

To my reader's group, *J. Nathan's Book Boyfriend Lovers*. Thank you for following me on this awesome book journey!

To my wonderful beta readers: Dali, Megan, and Maria. Thank you for always loving my books enough to read them when they're not perfect yet! Your feedback is what makes them their best! I always know I can rely on you!

To my editor Stephanie Elliot. Thank you for giving it to me straight. I know the first draft of this book was not my best work, but I hope you agree that it turned out so much better after *your* feedback.

To Kerrie and Amy for spending their days on the Cape coming up with ideas for this book! I hope I made you proud. Don't go anywhere. I'll need your help with my next book!! Love you both!!

To my wonderful PA Renee. Thank you for doing all the things for me. Keep being you because you're the best!

To Kate at Y'all. That Graphic. for creating another beautiful cover and amazing teasers! Thank you for putting up with my crazy need for things to be perfect.

To Michelle Lancaster for the gorgeous cover photo of Dylan. I hope you love the cover as much as I do!

A big thank you to Grey's PR for your assistance with this release! You are so wonderful to work with!

And, last but never least, thank you to my family and friends. I am so lucky to have your love and support! Nay, thank you for playing baseball and taking me to my first Cape Cod League game. It's where I got the inspiration for this book. Love you more than the universe!

www.ingramcontent.com/pod-product-compliance
Lightning Source LLC
Chambersburg PA
CBHW061526310726

48972CB00008B/2335